C000020181

MEMORY OF THE ABYSS

Marcello Fois

MEMORY OF THE ABYSS

Translated from the Italian by
Patrick Creagh

MACLEHOSE PRESS
QUERCUS · LONDON

First published in Italian as *Memoria del vuoto*
by Giulio Einaudi editore, Turin
First published in Great Britain in 2012 by

MacLehose Press
an imprint of Quercus
55 Baker Street
7th Floor, South Block
London W1U 8EW

A CIP catalogue record for this book is available
from the British Library.

ISBN 978 1 906694 00 5

10 9 8 7 6 5 4 3 2 1

Designed and typeset in Cycles by Libanus Press
Printed and bound in Great Britain by Clays Ltd, St Ives plc

To my father and mother,
because it is never too late

PART ONE

The Beginning of the Beginning

"How do you know you are not him?"
"Because I know I'm me!"
                    The Thousand and One Nights

Invocation and Protasis

Now grant me speech.

On the night of the killing, the full moon, fat and sweaty, had been squatting for hours on the crest of the mountains. A few wisps of cloud resembled unruly hair falling over its brow. Thus it hung, the moon, drinking from a horizon as jagged as the edge of an eggshell broken in two, indolent almost as death itself, as though in its first sleep.

Then, at a certain moment, it rose, stirring itself indolently upon the rim of the earth.

An ancient moon that, arching its back to stretch itself in the silence and tardily begin its round, had spread itself fully only to the eyes of the sleepless. Thus it had little by little shed a pallor on the landscape, igniting the phosphorescent hides of the livestock, making the blades of grass glitter like razors. It had moved across the vineyards, etching against the slab of the sky a black Golgotha of crucified plants. Then it entered the little town as if arriving by chance, an absent-minded traveller, lending a feverish light to the red roofs. It penetrated the mortar of the paved streets, turning them to precious silver, and selected pristine walls on which to reflect itself. It shed its light on orgasms, ah so it did! Both the lawful and the unlawful, with its white lashes wounding the flesh of lovers, piercing through the cracks in closed doors, worming its way though the chinks in curtains, darting between the slats of fastened shutters.

Further off, where the soil was always fat with worms,

it made the marble tombs shine like burning glasses, and felled to the ground the pitch-black shadows of slender cypresses standing to attention along the avenues, melting them onto the pavements. Ah, an accursed moon! That whispered of misfortunes, that night of the killing.

I

*In which it is related that a pair of boots can change the destiny of
a man, and that forewarnings often have an explanation, but are
no less important for all that. And where we tell of Samuele's
first separation and of lambs falling from the skies*

But years, many years before that night, there had been other
nights in Ogliastra. And other moons too. To tell of them all
would take many lifetimes. So we must concentrate on the one
on which, at the age of seven, I was walking along a road with my
father. He had been drinking and staggered a little, and laughed
at himself for his unsteady gait.

It was a Sunday, Saint Sebastian's Day.

We had been to a christening: the seventh son of Redento
Marras, and between this Redento and my father there was
holy oil, because the blacksmith of Elìni was godfather to my
elder brother Gonario. And I was wearing my brother's boots.

It happened like this. My father, Felice Stocchino, and my
mother, Antioca Leporeddu, had talked and talked about their
duty to be present at that christening, because Elìni was not
just round the corner from our house, it was a good four hours
on foot, and so on and so forth. And as if the matter of the
distance was not enough, there was the fact that they had
nothing to give the newborn babe to bring him luck on this
earth. And to bring luck on this earth you cannot turn up
empty-handed before one who has only just opened his eyes
to the world. No, no, not even the poorest shepherds arrived

empty-handed at the manger where Christ and the Madonna were.

In any case, my mother said there was no way out of it: a duty is a duty, the holy oil is too strong a bond. Not to attend the baptism of the seventh son of a god-relation is simply out of the question. It would be turning the world topsy-turvy. My father nodded, he did not deny it, but when you haven't got the needful you haven't got it and that is that. And even if they did have something to bring the infant, what about my brother Gonario, Redento's godson, who had grown out of his boots because his feet had got bigger by the day?

"Very well," says my father, "I have to take Gonario with me, but can I take him barefoot?" My mother and father exchanged a look.

"Take Samuele," says my mother, "because whether it's Gonario or Samuele it's all the same to Redento, who hasn't seen Gonario since the font . . . Those boots fit Samuele, so take Samuele with you."

Days such as that on which my parents agreed that I should go with my father to the baptism of Redento Marras' son are branded with the mark of destiny. One always thinks they are days like any others. But that is wrong, because things happen, and sometimes one sees things that ought not to happen or one ought not to see. So one tells oneself there's nothing strange about it, that everything is as usual, but that is not the case. For example, that very day, while my father and mother were trying to sort out the problem of the baptism, what should fall into the yard in front of my house but a lamb?

Just like that, out of the blue. As if a cloud had become so heavy that it crashed to earth and turned to pulp. We children were playing when we heard a great thump right behind us and Tzia

Mena shrieking. Then other people came running and they all gathered round to see the animal that had smashed to the ground.

Tzia Mena told the whole story. She was sweeping the yard, she stopped for a breather because her health is not what it was, then she heard a whistling sound, distant at first but then nearer and nearer . . . She looked up and saw that out of the skies, and she swears it by her children and grandchildren Amen!, that out of the skies a lamb was falling. It is as certain as certain that lambs don't fly, but it is equally certain that the creature splatted there on the ground had fallen from on high. "What do you mean, 'from on high'?" they began to ask. But Tzia Mena stuck to her guns: "Out of the sky, I tell you! From up there, from up above . . ."

It has to be said, though, that that woman was not a very reliable person . . . but let that go. However, they came to us children, me and Luigi Crisponi and Giuseppe Murru, and asked us what we had seen. Well, we had seen nothing, but heard something, that we had: a rushing of air and then a truly terrible sound, a dull thud, like a boulder falling in the distance or a sack of potatoes dumped heavily on the ground. Like when you slip and land up on your bum and before it starts to hurt you hear the sound of the bump. Yes, that's it: maybe that sound might best match the impossible idea of a land animal falling out of the sky. After all, the church was full of saints and lambs standing on clouds, and perhaps this particular animal had put a foot wrong. We all know, don't we, that although the clouds look solid they are tricking us. You have to watch your footing even in heaven, hanging there above the heads of us mortals. And we can add that at the Apocalypse, so they tell us, a whole lot of toads are waiting to fall from the skies onto the heads of sinners. So perhaps they were having a trial run . . .

The hubbub was at its height when Totore Cambosu arrived.

But he, a hunter who knows the secrets of nature, told everyone to calm down.

"This has nothing to do with saints or clouds, and not even with trial runs for the Day of Judgement. It's to do with birds of prey." When Totore spoke, dead silence fell. He bent down to examine the animal. "Hmm," he said, pointing at the lamb's white back on which some red scratches could be seen. "He grabbed it here and then he must have lost hold of it."

We all looked agog at Totore Cambuso. He is one of those who can bewitch you with the tales he tells.

The answer was simple enough. A golden eagle had picked a lamb out of the flock and carried it on high. The little creature had begun to struggle, its heart beating against its ribs and was so terror-stricken it could scarcely breathe. What's more, the air at that height is rarefied. All the same, from up in the sky the lamb could see huge things becoming tiny: the flustered shepherd rounding up the other lambs and shaking his stick in the air; the ram who, *conc'a susu*, was sniffing at the mistral; the maddened dog barking and leaping in an attempt to fly. Finally he saw his mother grazing away in the middle of the flock without a worry in her head, because since the world began it is always the meek who suffer. So if only for a moment the lamb knew what it was to fly, but then it realised that you need wings to be an eagle. So he tried to fly . . . Then it must have been that the eagle was young and had eyes too big for his stomach. So maybe he had not even realised that the lamb he had picked out was heavier than he had thought, all the more so because the creature in his talons was wriggling and wasn't helping at all, and so sensing that he would not manage to carry his prey all the way to the crest of the hill, he simply let go . . .

And the rest we know.

*

14

Then, amid all the confusion, along came Missenta Crisponi, afraid that her Luigi might have been up to something, and they told her about the lamb, so she turned to look at her son and went as white as a sheet, because we hadn't noticed but Luigi had a spot of the lamb's blood right in the middle of his forehead. So Missenda grabbed him, spat on a corner of her apron, rubbed vigorously with the damp material and wiped off the stain. Tzia Mena and the other women crossed themselves: *Sant'Antoni meu* . . . What on earth would happen next?

And how long was it, two days later? What should happen to Luigi Crisponi? He was a particular friend of mine, but his father died. He had seen very little of his father, perhaps only twice in seven years, maybe three times, who knows . . . ? But the fact of the matter is that when he was told his father was dead he could not even remember what he looked like. Yes, of course, Bartolomeo Crisponi was a tall man, but apart from that? Apart from that nothing, and when they asked him what his father was like he said he was tall and worked in a mine, and that was all. All the same Luigi felt it at once, for the odd thing is that even without a face to remember the grief is the same. Once Serafino Musu said to him that if he had nine brothers and sisters his father must have come home a few times, but Luigi gave him a perplexed look and I made a sign to Serafino to tell him to keep his mouth shut. This Serafino is older than us and knows a thing or two. So we decided not to go on about it, but Luigi insisted.

"You have all these brothers and sisters, so where do you think your mother found them?"

Luigi Cresponi looked this way and that, then clapped a hand over his mouth and opened his eyes wide.

Meanwhile, at Shaft Nine at Montevecchio they were bringing up the body of his father, four days dead. And that dead man's eyes were wide open too. As old people always say, when you die in the dark you look for the light. Destiny buried Luigi Crisponi's father before he died. Therefore, perhaps to keep at bay that terrible darkness and maybe also to alleviate the taste of caved-in earth that filled his mouth, he had opened his eyes wider than you can imagine, almost as if to pierce the close-woven fabric of the dark.

Brought home in a makeshift wooden coffin, the beanpole that had been Bartolomeo Crisponi arrived one January morning. The coffin was nailed up. But Missenta refused to sit there staring at a nailed-up coffin and asked them to open it, as she wanted to see her husband one last time. And the others were telling her to let it go, it was better to remember the living. Missenta nodded, but thought otherwise. She knew what she wanted and it was her business . . .

So they took off the coffin lid to show the dead man to his wife Missenta. Now that the blood had left him Bartolomeo's complexion was moon-like, almost shiny, as it had been when he was a boy: the smooth skin of a young girl.

Bartolomeo looked as if wearied by death, his eyes forced shut by the doctor at the mine, but still handsome. He was not even swollen. To all appearances he didn't even look dead. Austere, gaunt and massive, like a phosphorescent beech-tree trunk, like a discarded plaster cast. He could have been made of a material inert and organic at the same time, a huge pale larva, shining with its own light, wrapped in a dirty sheet.

Missenta looked fixedly at her husband, then at her neighbours, seeking their approval. As if to say: You understand, don't you, but in the state he is, his fingernails encrusted with earth, his face with the coal dust barely wiped off it, we can't bury this man. So the women laid him out on the kitchen table and undressed him.

Bartolomeo, naked as the first of men, was ready to receive

loving care. And the length of him! His legs stuck out over the edge of the table from the calf down. His feet were knobbly. Luigi Crisponi's mother wanted no-one else in the kitchen. She wanted to be with her dead husband's body. So the neighbours took the children home with them and fed them on bread and cheese and milk.

Once alone, Missenta began to examine that body which, though hers, had never really been hers. She did not think they had ever been more profoundly intimate, she and her husband, than at that moment, even though they had brought nine children into the world. She began to wash him with a lukewarm cloth. She was nervous but determined, lingering over details: the black nails, the coal dust in the wrinkles of his forehead.

When she had finished, she sat exhausted with her hands on her knees.

That inert, washed body all of a sudden gave her the measure of her sorrow. Which was terrible. And sharp. But it was also a profound and honest sorrow. Almost calm . . . As before an attack of vertigo. That instant of absolute stability, rather than peace, which comes before you fall. This was how she, Missenta Corrias, now the widow Crisponi, saw that sorrow of hers: as seriously as a sulky child.

Then she stood up. And as she did so a thought came into her head. Missenta bent towards her husband's mouth, to kiss it. Her lips brushed his, ice-cold but soft. Still with tiny traces of soil at the corners. Bartolomeo let her, and seemed languid and relaxed, seemed for once almost to like his wife's advances.

It was easy to kiss him: between the thought and the deed there came the perfect moment.

Then it happened.

Bartolomeo's eyelids suddenly shot open. His eyeballs were lifeless, his look was not a look, as if he were staring at some place unknown.

Missenta wanted to shriek, but what happened was worse. She felt dizzy, she was losing consciousness, she realised she was going to fall and fall she did. And in falling she grabbed hold of her husband's body and pulled it down on top of her.

Infernal racket! What horror can this be? *Per Deus e pe' santos*, what is happening? Someone knocked on the kitchen door: "*Missé* . . . open up for the love of God . . . *Missé*, what has happened?" But the woman was turned to stone, it was not even terror but something deeper, like a sense of eternal perdition. As when we slip and fall, in fact, and are not aware of falling but almost voluntarily let ourselves go just so as not to put it all down to chance. The naked body of her man covered her now with a shamelessness he had never had in life. Knocking and more knocking, but Missenta's thoughts were already drifting elsewhere . . . Try telling her now that Bartolomeo is dead. She'll never believe you, never, never, never . . .

The perfect moment. And the dizziness. Missenta's particular dizziness had endless explanations but only three names: dizziness, in fact, at the one instant when Missenta herself was able to think about it and thus give it a name; then, apoplectic fit, as Dr Milone said when he had inspected the body; while everyone else called it heartbreak.

In a word, when they broke down the kitchen door the only thing to be done was to order another coffin. Of the cheap kind.

Then it happened that one morning a bailiff turned up at the Crisponi place to tell them they had to get out of the house, that it did not belong to them, even if no-one knew to whom it did in fact belong.

That very night Luigi Crisponi had a dream.

He dreamed that he heard a terrible noise, really and truly an excruciating uproar, so he put his hands over his ears but, instead of stopping, the noise grew louder and louder. Then, in his dream, he was his father swallowed up by the earth. He was his father trying to cry out, but could only stare wide-eyed into the dark. You see, it was like what happens in visions, that someone honestly believes in what he dreams as if it were true. And in the power of that dream Luigi truly believed that he could not breathe and that there was no way at all to cleave that darkness. He believed that his father, to make up for all the gifts that he had never given him, had come to him in a vision to tell him of the thunderous horror of the long death he had died. It seemed to Luigi that he could see himself in the whites of his father's staring eyes that were the only source of light in that dense gloom. And it also seemed to him that that dream, persisting in him as both reality and its opposite, was a kind of trust which his dying father, his eyes staring, his mouth full of earth, grimed with coal dust, was bequeathing to him. Even if he, Luigi, could not say exactly what that bequest was.

Then it happened that no sooner did he awake than he stopped asking himself questions. He realised it was absolutely useless to lay claim to anything. He understood that his father's legacy was to be docile in the face of adversity . . . And he realised his mother had died for having put up a fight, for not having given way. She had died because she thought she could prevail over the destined course of her pointless existence.

Luigi thought, though not at once, indeed many years were to pass before he thought that a meaningful existence is purchased at the price of thousands of meaningless ones. His father had whispered this to him with the whites of his eyes, looking at him from the depths, from the foul bowels of mother earth.

And then, of course, troubles don't come singly . . . For not so much as a week had passed before they told Luigi that they were taking him to the orphanage in Cagliari. And he said he would escape and every time they caught him he would escape again. As for me, I almost wept.

It so happened that on the day he was supposed to be taken away Luigi had a high fever and the good neighbour who was looking after him was right there on her doorstep to tell the carabinieri that the child was ill, that looking after him was no trouble to her, that she scarcely thought he would be better cared for in an orphanage. But the carabinieri told her to wrap him up well, this Luigi Crisponi, son of the late Bartolomeo, because the law's the law and that is that.

So without more ado, I watched Luigi leaving from the window of my house and if my mother had not been at the window too I really would have cried. *Domo rutta*: an entire family vanished into nothing. But then the wheel spins, my mother said, and sooner or later even bad luck forgets you. But to a child the idea does not seem as clear as all that: I mean, the idea that bad luck every so often forgets you. That morning, standing at the window overlooking the Crisponi courtyard as they were taking Luigi away, I felt that there are separations as murderous as a pair of throttling hands. Then I thought of the treasure of tinfoil and bottle ends that we had buried only three steps away from the gate to Puddichinu's field, and the catapults to take potshots at finches with, and the time when our teacher Serusi had hung signs saying "WE ARE DUNCES" around our necks and made us parade all over the school, even to the girls' classes . . . The fact is, I thought the things one thinks when someone has died. And it is as if every separation were like grieving over a lost one.

It must be that I have never liked change. I have always been one of those who grow uneasy when faced by changes. My father thought this was because of my age. Yes, he said, I was still a child, but that even at seven years old one must have some idea about the world. But mine, he said, was not exactly an idea about the world, because the moment one comes to understand it, the world, that is, the first thing one realises is that it is all one long burial of the dead. Therefore, he said, I shouldn't worry my head, because what look like changes to a child are, once you grow up, always the same thing: being born and dying, and so on.

II

*In which is related a long journey on foot and, also,
what happened on the way back*

So came the day of the christening.

As a present my parents had bought on tick a measure
of coarse dark salt, a measure of coarse sugar and a measure of
coffee beans to roast. Just as Filomena Marras, Redento's wife,
had in her time. Because when you receive a present you are
obliged to return it later. Which, put like that, sounds almost as
if one gives a present only to get it back again, but it is simply
because one cannot arrive empty-handed to launch a new
baby. The point is that these occasions have to be honoured.
Honoured, as in Honour. And even if a person has nothing, he
always finds something with which to honour a christening, a
first communion, a confirmation, a wedding or a funeral, even
if he has to run up a debt as my parents did. And this is always
true, because it is one of those things that go without saying.

People who know wise things say that salt is the proof that the
sea breathes, for those not convinced by hearing it wheeze on
autumn nights. On its own, its taste is intolerable. It is a crystal,
a transitory, soluble gem.

Sugar is the proof of Eden. The fatal treasure. The one that
Adam lost. For those who do not believe there can be happiness
on earth. Out of the sweet came forth bitterness. Out of the
good came every ill. Sugar is crystal, a snowflake melted.

Coffee is the proof that we are the centre and the confines,

22

and within those confines there is another centre, and within that centre yet more confines. Coffee is the seed that travels over the oceans, where there are more centres and relentlessly more and yet more confines. Coffee is the gift of the toil of stooping women. It is dusty burned earth.

There: these are the terrible fruits of the blood, for the viaticum of the newborn babe.

So my brother's boots carried me a long way, to just outside Elìni, to Redento Marras' *tanca* where he was giving the party. And the party was an aroma that came to meet us, more than the babble of voices, more even than the laughter . . . It was the sweet-sour smell of meat from the centre of the open space where a charcoal fire lay dozing. Custodian cooks were roasting lambs and sucking pigs on the spit and swigging wine to counteract the heat. Then there were girls of marriageable age offering around baskets of pistachio nuts while mature women, mothers of families, poured steaming coffee.

Yes, everything had an odour and every odour wafted all around. Such a tasty odour, that just to sniff at it almost made a meal . . .

We reached the house. Filomena, Redento's wife, offered us a seat inside. She actually told us to sit down, because we must be tired: coming all that way on foot to honour them made it a double honour, she said. But we remained standing. Filomena repeated the invitation and I looked at my father. He gave me a nod and I sat down. Filomena looked hard at me and knitted her brow:

"Old friend," she said, turning to my father, "this is not Gonario!"

My father gave a nod in reply:

"With all respects, friend, and no offence meant, but Gonario's out with the sheep and we couldn't spare him from his work. He's already nine and has to do his bit for the family . . . As I couldn't bring Gonario I brought Samuele . . ."

Filomena scrutinised me as if she had to paint my portrait. "He's a handsome lad as well," she remarked to my father. Then she looked back at me: "Had anything to eat?" I shook my head.

And so to the feast.

We had witnessed the miracles of the loaves and the changing of the water into wine. The afternoon was drawing to a close among the blasphemous expletives of the *morra* players. At which point the master of the house poured my father another glass and said that as it was already getting dark, and for the child it was already late and seeing how far we had to go to get home, it was better we should stay there for the night.

"*No est pro cosa, ma est tardu pro su pitzinnu . . .*"

My father, looking around for me, knocked back his wine and said it was really too much trouble, and that anyway I wasn't a child; why, at seven he was already tending the sheep for Benedetto Mulas:

"*Itte pitzinnu e pitzinnu . . . Deo a s'edade sua . . .*"

"All the same, *compà*, it is better you stay over, that way we'll all be easier in our minds. Take my advice for once, there's room enough for you."

"*Compà*," said my father, "you very well know we're not going to fight over such matters. I cannot thank you enough, but if we don't get back Antioca will be worried. So now we'll be on our way and long life to the little one. *Adiosu.*"

And so saying, my father cut short the discussion and signalled to me to stop playing because we were leaving. We set off for home, me in my party togs and the boots that had been my brother's, and my father happily tipsy.

All along the village street were pasted "Wanted Persons"

posters. Those feverish faces, like the faces of martyrs, or in this case of bandits, watched us make our way out into the open country. Dead or alive as they might be. My father began to tell me about Giovanni Tolu, the bandit Epaminondas, whose mighty heart had held out against the assault of the new legal code, as the Spartan hero did against the Persians. He was as slippery as an eel whenever the police tried to grab him with their naked hands. And, far from being ferocious and bloodthirsty, he had forgiven more than he had condemned. He, Giovanni Tolu from Florinas, when they tried to catch him in nets had turned himself into air, and into water when they tried to force him out with fire. He, Giovanni Tolu, the man who refused to die, had put down roots in our flesh like an age-old tree. So said my father, who had met him as an old man.

Meanwhile the night came galloping towards us between the oak trees of Santa Barbara, and the moon burst out from the sea out beyond Tortolì. And there was a long way to go! "Your mother won't let us into the house," said my father, stamping his heavy boot on the parched earth. Then he laughed.

It was cold that night of Saint Sebastian, martyr of the faith, bound to a pillar and pierced through and through by the emperor's archers. Because, my father said, justice dwells in the houses of the rich. And the black bread kind of faith, that of simple folks, is only a forgotten tale.

Walking in the clear moonlight we reached the house of Emerenziano Boi, the cooper. A dim light from his windows told us he was still at work. My father knocked three times, as wayfarers do. He asked for water.

"This time of night I don't open the door to anyone," shouted the cooper from within. "Not even if you were the Apostles themselves, I wouldn't open up," he repeated.

Whereupon my father gave his name and patronymic, so he would know who he was: "Stocchino Felice di Bernardo de sos

25

de Crabile," he said. "I want water for the child, he's thirsty, we're on our way back from the christening of Redento Marras' newborn son, a fine lad to be sure, God bless him . . ."

"Go to the stream," said the cooper.

"That's another hour on foot," objected my father.

"No-one ever died for the sake of an hour," said the other and doused the light.

My father spat on the ground. "I'll make it, I'll make it," I said and started towards home. My father did not move. He seemed to be waiting for something that he knew would never happen. Then he spat on the ground again and, with the toe of his boot, made a sign on the ground in front of the cooper's door.

Describing that night it seems like nothing much, because nights cannot be described. One cannot describe the pungent odours of plants as they shake off the light of the day just past; the smell of the animals roving in search of food. Nor can one describe the sound of olive berries shaken to the ground by the petulant tramontana. Beyond description even the sharp sound of our footsteps on the rutted roadway, with each step raising a cloud of dust as red as the breath of Lucifer when he realised he was falling. Each night is a maelstrom, a breathless plunge, a memory of the abyss.

We walked in silence, straining our ears in an effort to hear the sound of running water before we got to it. I was terribly thirsty, but I said nothing for fear of angering my father . . .

That night resounded like a tin roof, beyond the mountains, far out over the sea, Su Tumbarinu was drumming up a storm. We heard it, muffled by distance, as if we were a couple of outsiders hearing the laughter and the dancing at a party. That sort of sadness changes the world, turns the world upside down like the hand of God scooping up an enormous cowpat. As a ploughshare does, creating waves of earth.

And then we saw the stag.

My father was walking head down, chewing bad temper like the cud. I had slipped a hand into his pocket and he had put a hand over mine. "Not far now," he murmured. The wine had evaporated from his brain and given place to sullen rancour. In his hand I could feel the fierce thudding of his heart. "Not even water," he muttered to himself. "Not even water . . ." So then we saw the stag. Glistening like a precious stone. I felt my father check his steps, so I looked up and saw it. The animal turned his head too and looked at us as if aware that in that gaze of his was all the nobility of the centuries, as if he were a spirit bearing tidings. "I was expecting you," said that look, "you, Felice, and you, Samuele, I was expecting you." That look spoke of blood and sorrow, exactly like the Angel of the Annunciation who foretold the Seven Sorrows of the Blessed Virgin.

It was then that my father put his hand over my eyes. In that warm darkness I learned my destiny: solitude, the death of affection, the snarl of vengeance.

This happened on the night of 20 January, 1902. The following morning Gesuina Lindiri, the widow Boi and mother of the cooper, stepped out of the house. In her apron she carried grain for the hens and potato peelings for the pigs. A ferocious wind gave no respite, the leaves were whistling like whiplashes. A gust caught her headscarf and she tried to grab at it, letting go of her apron and spilling the contents all over the yard: the grains swirled around as if tracing an invisible spiral, the peelings hung in the air a moment before tumbling to the ground. Old Gesuina, scarcely more than a bag of bones, was almost bowled over. She only just had time to grab at a ring fixed to the wall of the house, one of those used for tethering animals. Away flew the shawl, abandoned to its fate. Bare-headed as a penitent, with her skirts up and clinging to her body, the woman looked all around her: it was a blue-black morning. Gesuina crossed herself. Then she saw the mark. An "S" traced on the ground.

III

Which tells how Antioca finds she is pregnant for the fourth time
and implores the Virgin not to let her have more children

Antioca Leporeddu, wife of Felice Stocchino, rose early on
15 August, 1894. She was well aware of what she had done a
few nights before, of what she had allowed to happen. And now
she had decided to take measures. There was a chill in the air
in spite of its being mid-August, but old people say it is the
weather on Assumption Day that tells you how the cold season
will be. So there was reason to expect a biting winter. The sky
was leaden, like the surface of a smoky old wooden spoon. Not
even the birds were singing yet. And the moon seemed to be
melting. Veiled like the Virgin herself. So complete was the
silence she felt the urge to cry out. No sound even of breathing
from the room in which her sons were sleeping. All held their
breath, even the earth was holding its breath. Even the leaves.
Antioca heard nothing but the beating of her own heart. To
calm herself she heaved a sigh, but it was no good . . . She opened
the chest where she kept the only good dress she had. She laid
it out on the kitchen table like the mortal remains of a dear
departed. She washed herself by wetting a rag in a bucket of
water, undressing bit by bit because she was shy even of the
sight of her own body. After washing her top half she undid her
nightdress and let it fall to the ground. When she removed
her knickers she saw something that she did not like at all:
the strip of cloth between her legs was all too clean. Antioca
Leporeddu, devoted wife and mother, counted on her fingers to

make a primordial calculation. But without bringing in mathe-
matics, she knew the perfect workings of nature. Therefore
what she had decided on had to be done.

By the time she woke Genesia, her elder daughter, she
was already fully dressed, with her plait tied with ribbons and
her headscarf neatly arranged. She looked almost beautiful, did
Antioca, in her best dress.

"Wake up, you've work to do," she said in a loud whisper
to Genesia.

"Eh?" Genesia gawped at her as if at a stranger, thinking
for a moment that it was a fine lady tapping her on the
shoulder.

"Eh, eh," echoed Antioca. "I'm off. I've left you everything
ready in the kitchen."

Genesia's eyes were sticky with sleep. "But where are you
going?" she mumbled.

"There's something I have to do. Let your father have a
lie-in, he doesn't often get the chance." Genesia nodded, but
then it seemed to sink in. "What shall I tell him if he asks?"
said she, sitting up in bed.

"Tell him I've gone with the priest's party to Orgosolo for
the celebration of the Assumption."

"You said you were going to take me with you," Genesia
said sulkily, only then realising what time and what day it was.

"Yes, yes, but then how would they manage here . . . ? I've
left everything ready. I'll be back this evening. And mind your
brother because he'll eat you out of house and home if you let
him, And don't put cheese in your father's broth because you
know he doesn't like it." Genesia gave a nod. She realised that
some unspoken worry lay behind her mother's instructions.
"Make sure you all have a good wash," she went on. "Not like
usual, as if you were cats."

By now Genesia was on her feet, and the floor resounded

29

to the sleepy rhythm of the awakening house. A pale, pale dawn was in the making.

Antioca left the house as though fleeing from herself. Once outside those walls she became another person, one who knew what she was about. There in the house nothing had seemed possible. Now, as she hurried to reach the church steps, everything seemed to be true. And right and proper.

The first mail coach for pilgrims to the Assumption had already left. But there was still the ox-cart that would reach Orgosolo in five or six hours, in time for the procession. Nine women climbed aboard the cart. Antioca was the tenth.

The darkness dissolved soon after the cart had passed the public wash-trough. Maybe even swallowed up in that mirror of insect-buzzing water. Now every sound could be heard: the shod hooves of the oxen, the squeak of the metal rims fitted to the cart to modernise it and absorb the worst bumps in the road. But not sufficiently: that precarious perch on the seat, that discomfort, that whole rough, bumpy journey, appeared to Antioca as a foretaste of the omnipotence of the Blessed Virgin, who had understood the sword that was piercing her through.

But the road was long. An unspeakable torment of jolts and lurches! A continual shriek from the metal-plated parts of the cart. Jolt after hellish jolt, heading north-west.

"We're going to take the road by Corr 'e Boe," said the ox-cart driver. The priest had woken him up in the middle of the night to tell him the mail coach was full, and had begged him to take the stranded pilgrims. "Have you brought things to wrap up in? It's as cold as the devil up there. Even now in August there's not a thing growing."

Legend has it that there has never been a springtime at Corr 'e Boe. Just autumns and winters. The women told him, yes, do take that route if it's shorter . . . But really there wasn't much of a choice. Either you made for the sea or for the mountains. If you took the first option it meant an hour or two of comfortable travel, then up and down and some really steep passes. Because when you say "to the sea" you don't exactly mean the sea, but the mountains that loom above it. So you are still high in the mountains even if you have only to look down to catch a glimpse of the beaches. If you made for the mountains the agony was evenly distributed throughout the journey. As in life. A slow, steady climb, then a descent from the hills to the plain, and then another climb . . .

The women told him, yes, they had things to wrap up in.

Antioca was watching the earth giving birth to the light. Such was her heartache that it left her almost breathless. Tossed about in the tumult of bushes desiccated by an unseasonal frost; with the smell of already-dry leaves pounded to dust beneath the heavy wheels and the hoofs of the oxen.

"A pity about the rosary," said one of the women.

"Yes, but by now we can say it for ourselves, can't we?" said another.

"Ah, but with Father Marci with us it was a different thing," insisted the first.

"Eh, eh," said a third. "It's not even a good thing for the soul to think such things."

"I know what you mean," the first woman was forced to admit, "but all I meant was that it's a shame we couldn't go with the mail coach as we did last year . . . It was fun and it took no time at all . . ."

Their voices were like buzzing bees. To Antioca everything seemed foreign. There were two of Antioca, as we've already said. There was the fearless one, able to look at the frightened one as if she were hovering just above her head. Antioca raised her eyes. The talk of the other women, lively at first, had little by little dwindled away into silence.

31

Antioca and Antioca therefore began to converse.

"Shame on you," said the one to the other, "you've let yourself get pregnant like a low woman. What did you think, that it was up to the man to say no?"

"You bitch!" said the one to the other. "You bitch, bitch and bitch again."

"Good for you," said the fearless persona. "So you're making this pilgrimage, but it won't do you a bit of good, because when things are written they are written and that's the end of it. It's not in your power to change them."

"If the Blessed Virgin wishes to help me, she will – she will look on me with compassion . . .".

"She has better things to do than to look after bitches on heat . . ."

"No, no! She hears even one's heartbeat, even one's sighs, she hears the least whisper . . . and she turns to look."

"Shame on you, shame on you Antioca Leporeddu, you've let yourself be trapped like a rat . . . Ha, ha, ha!"

Antioca gestured as if to brush away the sound of that mocking laughter. The women in the cart gave her enquiring looks.

"Our Lady knows what we are asking in our hearts," she said out of the blue in answer to a question that had not been asked.

"Amen," nodded the women.

"Wrap up warm, because I don't want any problems," said the carter.

Antioca and the other women covered their heads and wrapped their shawls around them, covering their mouths. God willing they'll stop blabbering, thought the carter.

In the warmth of her breath her thoughts mingled together to no effect. A stubborn somnolence overcame her eyelids. The lurch of the cart was tough on the back and her head seemed too heavy to hold upright. Her chin propped on her chest, Antioca let herself go . . .

"I don't want more children, I don't want them, you, Holy Mother of us, you know why I am here. You alone know. And if you can see me, if you deign to see me in the multitude of souls who are beseeching you, then grant my wish, for I do not, do not want another child . . ."

And the Blessed Virgin, identical in every way to the one in the parish church of Arzana, though without the jewels donated by the faithful, sat down beside her in the cart and put a loving arm around her shoulder. Antioca felt a warmth that spread to her very loins.

"I am here," said the Virgin, "and among the immense multitude of beseeching souls I have chosen you, Antioca Stocchino born Leporeddu. I have chosen you in order to tell you that three more swords will transfix you. And to tell you that this child you carry in your womb will be both your joy and your anguish. And to tell you that because of this, my chosen suffering creature, you are especially dear to me. And also to tell you that I love even your doubting and even your anger."

Creaturedda iscaminada
in su bentu 'e su destinu,
a ti torrare in caminu
deo pro custu so falada

chanted the Virgin who, perpetually lit by Pentecostal flames, can speak in all the tongues that may be spoken.

Antioca wept quietly in her sleep. The women in the cart exchanged glances and shook their heads.

"Why make me bring other suffering creatures into the world?" she asked.

The Virgin smiled, exactly as in the old bound and illustrated missal. "Little soul, poor in spirit," she smiled, "I love you and you are dear to me . . . I am here because everything has a meaning, I am here to tell you that you are part of a perfect

33

design. Of course, Antioca Stocchino born Leporeddu, in the immense picture you are a mere dot, a dot within a dot, the tip of the smallest blade of grass in a vast meadow, a meadow which is itself infinitesimally small. Do you understand, my suffering creature?"

In her sleep Antioca seemed to nod her head.

"Therefore," said the Virgin, caressing the nape of her neck, "go, and do not ask for what you wish for, but try to wish for what has been assigned to your lot. Go, and accept the cup that is offered to you, for without this unconditional acceptance the world would be only a place of the walking dead . . . Here now, I will breathe into your ear as the warrior Archangel did into mine. And this breath is a soul that enters into your flesh. Now you are the emblem of life, O suffering creature; you are the emblem of our journey through this vale of tears. What is called life is nothing but a brief sojourn in the womb of earth. Being born is all the rest . . ."

When Antioca opened her eyes the cart was turning from Pratobello towards Orgosolo. Pilgrims on horseback were hastening towards the sanctuary of Our Lady of the Assumption. It was a pallid day, the sun obscured by an overcast sky. Silent flocks were grazing on the high plateau. The cart began the descent towards the ridge, virtually a granite outcrop where the grey village perched. Now that the crowds were gathering the women had to leave the cart and continue on foot.

They then went on to watch the passage of the Sleeping Virgin, who ascended into heaven after a long sleep that is death, but only apparently so, because death does not exist. They attended the exposition and the procession so that every one of them could see and weep. And ascertain what portion of the grand design they were a part of. Let them weep indeed and let them remember! As every day one feeds on flesh and blood, thus, during the rite, though hastily accomplished in scarcely more than the instant of her passing by, they must remember from what mystic source that flesh and blood sprang forth. And perhaps those who ought to remember do not remember, and perhaps it is only a mere gesture and a glance: the border of the veil that covered the sleeping statue; the sky-blue mantle; the whiteness of the robe . . . And maybe beneath the veils of the soul the body takes up too much room and weighs upon the earth. But this is so in the theatre of man. Death, which does not exist, we never get inured to, it is a constant, age-old sorrow that has dug deep furrows in the rock which is us. Maybe because the public procession, the public lamentation, which is always silent, is accompanied by our own sorrow and weeping. This is why we want to remember, so as not to let unreason win the day. And there in procession, there in the theatre of the tormented body, in the embrace given to her suffering children, we lay our burden down. Die for us, we cry in silence. And walking as lightly as in a dance, we will be able to defend the flank of that sorrowful multitude who, the wide world over, grieve in the selfsame manner.

When the effigy of the Sleeping Virgin passed close to her and a light breeze lifted the veil from the face, Antioca tucked a lock of hair back under the tight rim of her headscarf, then stroked her belly . . .

IV

Some premonitions about the coming baby and
a few scraps of gossip

That he would be called Samuele was decided by Father Marci:
"Samuele was one of God's knights. The fact is that every
time the Children of Israel failed to keep the Covenant which
they had made with God, which was to honour him above all
things, God allowed them to be enslaved by other peoples until
they repented. So a few years later, for God is very merciful, he
took pity on his children who had been reduced to slavery
and remembered that a Covenant was a Covenant, so he sent
a knight full of the Holy Spirit to rescue them. And the most
shining of his knights was the Prophet Samuel. God had asked
him to go and summon the King he had elected for his Chosen
People. So Samuel anointed the brow of a young man called
Saul. But this Saul did not turn out to be the right person. He
became proud of himself and forgot that it was God who had
made him king . . .

"So God once more turned his back on his People who were
enslaved again. Therefore the good man Samuel besought him
to return and look upon his people, and the terrible sufferings
they were undergoing for having forgotten the Covenant they
had made with him. And God, who is immeasurably good, was
once more moved to pity for all those men and women and
little boys and girls. So he asked Samuel to go to Bethlehem and
seek out a very pious youth, a shepherd by the name of David.
Exactly . . . him of Goliath, but that is another story. I have told

you this story for you to know who Samuel was: a very good man and very, very beloved of God. You will see that that is no small matter . . ."

Felice bowed his head and wrung his cap in his hands:

"With all due respect," he murmured, "we had thought of calling him Basilio."

Father Marci spread his arms.

"I understand," he assured him. "It means that if it is a girl you will call her Basilia after her dear-departed grandmother . . . But if it is a boy the name is Samuele."

"Who knows if it's a boy or a girl . . . ? It's just that we felt badly about not honouring my mother-in—"

"Believe me, your mother-in-law understands everything from where she is on high, so you can keep it for your next child," broke in Father Marci, full of enthusiasm. Then after a moment or two, noticing Felice's blank face, he changed tone. "And what's all this about? Is this the last child you're thinking of having? God forbid!" he thundered. "It isn't as if procreation was for you to decide, Felice Stocchino!"

"Well, write it down for me, this name, because I don't want to get it wrong with the town clerk," said Felice, defeated.

On 20 May, 1895, Father Marci was thereby enabled to write SAMUELE STOCCHINO in nice big letters for the benefit of the town clerk.

When Samuele was born his grandmother Basilia, his mother's mother, had been dead for five months. She had died on the very night of Christmas Eve. Antioca went into silent mourning for thirty days, dressed in black from head to foot, as did her two growing daughters Genesia and Ignazia. She made black armbands and buttonholes for Felice and Gonario. Her vow of silence was almost a blessing, for in the short time it had taken that ravenous sickness to carry off Basilia she, Antioca, had done

37

nothing but talk the whole time. Away from home while hearing of strange losses of appetite such as had come upon Basilia. At home with her friends, describing how one morning the old woman had said "I don't feel well" for the first time. In church, praying for her to get better, or at least to grant her the time to see this new grandchild who was thriving and healthy; until it occurred to her that it was more realistic to beg for time until the Christmas festivities were over. She talked as she had never talked in her life before, did Antioca, to find a way of keeping at bay the fearful terror that engulfed her. She talked and talked even to herself, remembering the three swords foretold to her by the Virgin in her dream.

When someone talks in this way surely it is to give some meaning to her bewilderment. Or to fill the void which anguish scoops out within you.

Five months before, therefore . . . It was Christmas Eve.

Doctor Milone emitted a fragrance such as never was, like a kind of wafting sanctity, as he brought the masculine, angelic face of a Saint Michael sacrificing himself to visit the dying woman even on a day of rest, constructing a smile such as to penetrate the bushy eyebrows of an Antioca who did not implore, nor even question. She seemed simply to be thinking. She seemed like a penitent pilgrim standing before the marble statue of a saint. But it is not certain that all that sheen emanating from the doctor was really marble; it might have been some natural reflection which drank in light and then diffused it all as some soft and cottony substance. This daughter of Eve did not ask for a miracle. All Antioca asked for was a little respite, she had always known that it is no good asking a favour when the verdict has already been pronounced. But it was Christmas Eve, so could not this be the very day for a miracle to happen? No, no, on the contrary, this was rather the proper day to make a good death. Otherwise Doctor Milone simply advised them to have plenty to eat, although he did not mention what there might actually be in the Stocchini larder. Thereupon, with the slight impatience of one in the know, the doctor bent over the patient, brushed her hand for an instant . . . But Basilia was already lost in a place of no return. Doctor Milone turned to face Antioca. The silence in the room felt strange, because everyone knew it was a place normally full of voices. But by this time the youngsters had gone off, Gonario and Ignazia to tend the sheep, Genesia to her job as a maidservant to Notary Porceddu. Felice stood in the background, ready to make himself scarce when the women arrived, because the dying woman had to be changed. Now that the house had become the antechamber to a long farewell, a Purgatory on earth, at last there was silence. Yes, a silence that was already death.

The doctor, however, did not give up: they should try to make this time of waiting holy, they should accept the gift of a truce . . . "After all, she's not going to die tonight," hazarded the doctor with a smile. In reply Antioca simply compressed her lips. They remained there for endless seconds face to face, until the sainted healer straightened his neck in a gesture of goodbye. As he left he felt the woman's gaze plastered to his back, but he did not turn.

Felice stood there for a while, wondering whether Doctor Milone would give him a glance before vanishing through the door. He did not. Weeping, perhaps, and imploring him might have given some meaning to his day, and even bawling and throwing things around can make one more light-hearted. But Felice was never light-hearted. Despite his name, he bore within him all the weight of the centuries. To him silence said everything. For silence speaks, but you must know how to listen to it. Silence was for him like a person always looking at you, never taking his eyes off you. If you steal, for example, silence is watching you. And no matter if it does not speak. The point is not that it cannot tell anyone what you are up to. The point is that it watches you, and the eyes of silence are terrible! They are not amiable like those of the doctor, who on the contrary had the gift of words to explain things. But what can you say about a woman who is dear to you, eaten away by cancer? What is there to say? And then the rest of it, all the rest . . . There too silence dogged him, during the desperate hours with Antioca falling into sudden fits of grief, and then there was this creature about to come into the world. It was all too difficult. Even though through silence itself Felice understood that there was a precise design in this tribulation, and maybe if one could express it well, pronounce every syllable of it, call it by name, everything would suddenly become easier . . . But how to find the right words?

To Antioca it seemed that now, sitting face to face at the table in their silent kitchen, she and Felice were more alone than ever. Worse than in the empty corridor of a hospital in Nuoro, far from home, or worse still Sassari, which is at the end of the earth. They were much more alone living this mockery of normality. In the suffering of the rooms of the dying a person feels so immersed in the mud of the approaching death that he almost seems happy. But outside those rooms everything has already been, or else does not exist. So that means that problem does not exist. That Purgatory is almost as bad a thing as can happen to one, almost worse than the weeks of waiting for the medical report that announces the end. The End that has a beautiful face, and one might say that it should never, never . . . come to an end. The End has a faint, faint voice, with scarcely the breath to say yes or no. That kind of end has the appearance of an answer, as if to say that the long suspended bridge you are on is crossed, with its swinging and swaying. The hazardous chasm is behind you. The end is that you have no time to glory in the answer before you have to face reality. Maybe that is why

Antioca thought to herself that everything solid and masculine has an end. Whereas the end itself is feminine. Everything has an end, she said to herself . . . The end itself has an end. And beyond that we cannot go.

So Samuele was born in May, which is the month of the Virgin Mary. The month of roses and weddings. Of bursting into bloom. Of the fullness of spring, for those who can afford it. Weighed on scales intended for sacks of potatoes, he turned out to be 2.9 kilograms, which for a boy baby is not any great weight. But he was healthy, thanks be to God, and so hungry that he sucked until it hurt, the little devil. His eyes were an unusual, almost amber colour, like arbutus-berry honey. Antioca looked at him as at one she feared. She knew the reason why. She knew it . . .

Maybe this is why Samuele grew up a little spoilt. In so far as it is possible to grow up spoilt in a family as poor as dirt.

Samuele and his mother were engaged in a continuous conversation. It was as if every time she looked at him she remembered how resolved she had been not to have him and that he, with equal resolve, wanted to remind her how determined he was to survive.

Such as that time when Samuele was two years old and they went together to the public wash-trough. Ignazia had been carried off by gastroenteritis a few months earlier. Samuele had a curly head like that of a little prince, very clean and tidy. Antioca pulled him behind her entangled in her skirts, the basket of laundry balanced on her head and with the posture that entails. A caryatid and a little Cupid. Samuele was well built, delicate but not frail. Well, the little boy started playing very close to a slippery patch of ground, his mother pulled him back, and he turned and gave her a look. That look froze all the women there. A look full of suffering and reproach. It was the look of an old man who has a long story to tell. Anníca Tola, who can see into people's very breasts, stared at him a moment and then crossed herself.

All the way home Antioca said not a word, and Samuele seemed to have returned to being the child he was, or perhaps was not as yet. That moment when his eyes gave expression to the rancour of centuries seemed quite forgotten. But Antioca did not forget and on that return journey with Samuele her last-born, she chewed a bitter cud.

It was a few days later, who knows how many, when right outside the cemetery gates Anníca Tola, spotting Antioca alone without the child, stopped to have a word with her.

"In the name of the souls in Purgatory and of all the saints," she said, "I saw it all." Antioca knew what Anníca was capable of seeing, because on other occasions when it had happened she had been able to confirm that she really had the gift. This time, however, she just did not want to hear. But Anníca persisted: "*Sorre cara*", she said. "Listen to me, and don't block your ears and your mind like that."

Antioca was in fact holding her hands over her ears, like a child afraid of too dreadful a revelation. But Anníca was right about one thing: you can stop up your ears, but not your mind.

"That child has a heart shaped like the head of a wolf," Anníca burst out. "He has the jagged sort of heart that murderers have." Antioca stabbed a sharp finger at her, but she knew she was fighting a losing battle. Anníca had seen a monkey's head in the chest of Filippo Tanchis and in fact it soon became plain enough that he was mad. She saw a fish-shaped heart beneath the ribs of Elène Cancellu and in fact she turned out daft. Once, when she was young, she had even seen her own heart while looking in the mirror, and had seen it had the shape of a jug, and so she knew what curse she had been afflicted with. "*Sorre cara*, not even I am happy about it. Accursed be the hour when I learned I could look into the hearts of others."

But Antioca did not give up and continued to say it wasn't true, and the more she said it the more evident it became that Anníca was right. Anyway, how else could it be? She had prayed for the child not to be born: "To be born into all this desperation one really does need the heart of a wild beast!"

Anníca shook her head. "No," she said, "these things do not happen according to what we humans want. Do not get above yourself, Antioca. The question of children doesn't depend on the mothers, it's only a question of destiny. God dispenses hearts shaped like the heads of wolves or monkeys or fish in the breasts of certain people because they are hearts without choice, with their fate already written. Criminal, mad, simple-minded. To make it clear to all the others, whose hearts are fist-shaped, how lucky they are to be able to choose. Then to some people Our Lord gives jug-shaped hearts, which is the worst of all, because they fill up only to empty again, they fill up but cannot stay full." By now the sky was divided in half: leaden on one side, blue on the other. The sun had been blocked out, forming a solid shadow. Anníca drew a smooth pebble from her apron pocket. "Your son's heart is no bigger than this," she said, showing it to Antioca. "It's a puppy, it's jumping about uncontrollably, it doesn't know its own strength . . ."

"What must I do?" asked Antioca.

"What must you do, dear neighbour?" replied Anníca with a shake of the head. "Hide this pebble in a place only you know about and as long as it is hidden that heart will not grow, the fangs will remain milk-teeth, the eyes will be gentle . . ."

With grief beyond words Antioca turned towards home. She had only to raise her eyes to see that the sky had turned livid like a bruise.

She made her way home and found Samuele playing in the yard, bending down to look at a caterpillar. She barely gave him

43

a nod as she entered the house. She went straight to the room with the chest which had been Basilia's (God rest her), opened it and dug her hand in under the linen to hide the pebble Anníca had given her. Down there, between two sheets of tissue paper, was the apron and bodice she kept for "best". Antioca put the pebble under the bodice, which was almost at the bottom of the chest, but above the linen towels . . . Then she had to shut the lid quickly because out in the yard Samuele was crying and Genesia was howling . . .

In the yard a tragedy had taken place. Samuele had squashed the caterpillar and flung the corpse into Genesia's hair, and now she was frantically trying to shake it out. Samuele was laughing fit to bust. The lovely laughter of a two-year-old child . . .

But that night Samuele had a terrible dream. Even though he was too young to have dreams of that kind.

It was about a beast, a huge bird with a long hairy neck. As ugly as the devil. It had two wrinkly claws and a round, feathered body too hideous for words. And it was a flightless bird, because in the dream Samuele, no longer a child but a grown-up, was chasing it and it was running, not flying. Samuele was alone in the middle of a field, a grown man but also a child dreaming all this. At a certain moment the beast spoke to him. "You will be a snake and a serpent," it told him. "You will be lauded and martyred. You will be the devil, cursed Satan himself. Drenched with blood and immaculate as a lily." This is what it told him.

"Who are you?" asked the grown-up Samuele. But the beast simply looked at him. A wide beak and protruding eyes . . . It was like a sea monster, only on land . . . That's what it was like. But it stared at him and, without moving its beak, told him that he could not ask questions, that an end had come to all questions. An end to everything that can be asked. "But I'm not saying anything or asking anything," murmured Samuele.

"Your very life is a question," said the beast, rolling those eyes like two glass marbles too big for its head. Its tongue flickered in and out like a purple worm . . . Then it came towards him as if to peck his face . . . Ahh . . .

When he got home from the christening party Samuele could not get to sleep. Accompanied by Antioca's quivering rage the two wayfarers were delivered from the darkness to the faint flame of the kitchen fireplace. Everyone else in the house was sleeping. Felice was simply not up to facing Antioca's querulous resentment, so he set off for bed without listening to her. For the brief time left to him he fell into a restless sleep. He had said nothing to his wife about the cooper and the water he had refused them. Samuele watched but said nothing. To Antioca the look in his eyes was still that fierce look seen at the wash-trough. For her Samuele was like a bottomless abyss. She would have liked to have hugged him but was waiting for permission from his eyes. She would embrace him if he wanted.

"Go to bed," she said.

Samuele took off his jumper and shoes.

Then he was alone in his bed in the kitchen. Around him the house was at last breathing the intangible repose of weary bodies. And the darkness of a black moon darted shafts of mad dogs and sleepless birds and ferrets into the woods . . . It was a darkness that seethed like a can of worms. That silence, which is the realm of expectations, of rustlings and vibrations, of snaps and murmurs, filled his head with thoughts. He did not even have the words to say all that should be said, but as far as he could tell everything, everything had been said already. Of the certainty of that Samuele had but a deaf, dumb, blind awareness. Therefore, to seek a key to unlock the mysterious casket containing everything that has already been, Samuele went and sat on the windowsill facing out onto the mourning of the moon. He

45

was seven years old and he had so many questions to ask. But the beast in his dream, all that time before, had told him that he could not ask questions . . .

The windowsill was a low one, a little jump was enough, then six or seven paces and the landscape swallowed him up.

This happened on the night of 20–21 January, 1902.

The following morning Gesuina Lindiri, the widow Boi and mother of the cooper, stepped out of the house. In her apron she carried grain for the hens and potato peelings for the pigs. A ferocious wind gave no respite, the leaves on the trees were whistling like whiplashes. A gust caught her headscarf and she tried to grab at it, letting go of her apron and spilling the contents all over the yard: the grains swirled round as if tracing an invisible spiral, the peelings hung in the air for a moment before tumbling to the ground. Old Gesuina, scarcely more than a bag of bones, was almost bowled over. She only just had time to grab at a ring fixed to the wall of the house, one of those used for tethering animals. Away flew the shawl, abandoned to its fate. Bare-headed as a penitent, with her skirts up and clinging to her body, the woman looked all around her: it was a blue-black morning. Gesuina crossed herself. Then she saw the mark. An "S" carved into the ground.

That morning there was no sign of Samuele in the bed in the kitchen. Call him as they might, there was no answer. The name Samuele echoed and re-echoed among the sapling oaks and wild olives. Felice and the menfolk clambered over the frost-slicked rocks, searching almost to the very foot of Monte Idolo . . . In the village the women were knocking at all the doors, raging and desperate, with all the grief that is in mothers and all the vexation of grandmothers.

"How could you have left the child unguarded, you foolish virgins, you senseless mothers! Ah, you wretches!"

"What do you mean *child*?" raged Felice in the fury of the

46

hunt. "Me, at his age I was . . . Just wait till I lay my hands on him . . ."

So while Antioca was suffering the humiliation of an irresponsible mother, Felice was looking forward to that spanking, he would show him . . . Meanwhile they searched in every nook and cranny, they searched in caverns where the air was as bitter as chicory. They searched from house to house, with a desperation that verged on resignation.

Samuele. That name cleft the silence, split the heart in two. As if the heart were a loaf of bread to be shared around.

"Mary Virgin, Our Lady of Heaven . . ." murmured Antioca, not in prayer but in panic.

She battered at the doors of Caterina Frangipane, Nicchedda Sale, Gerolama Filigheddu and Luisedda Pische . . . And all of them with one accord crossed themselves nose to chin and said no, they hadn't seen Samuele. But they might ask around . . . What anguish, what a cross to bear! Poor thing, with that son . . .

Antioca arrived panting at the house of Anníca Tola and found her waiting on the doorstep.

"Sister dear, sister dear," she said. She was watching a scene that she knew well, she had seen so many people fighting against their own destiny that she could not even count them. "Have you kept the stone I gave you?" she asked Antioca.

Antioca nodded, then had second thoughts and ran back home. Opening the chest she thrust aside the good clothes preserved in bags of lavender and wild onion. At the bottom, under the bodice, the stone was there alright. But it had split in two.

In the meantime, Gesuina Lindiri was frantically trying to erase the mark made on the ground by Felice Stocchino's boot. But she could not. That mark seemed to have been hewn into the very rock beneath the topsoil.

47

The cooper himself, seeing her there on all fours scraping at the ground with her fingernails, went and took hold of her to help her to her feet, but his old mother would have none of it: "Do you know what this wind means?" she asked.

Emerenziano Boi, fourth generation of coopers, said that, yes, it had been a storm, a passing storm, but now it was all over. Gesuina shrugged her son's hands from her shoulders and said that, no, it was not all over, it was just about to begin.

V

Samuele in the abyss

The rock walls outlined a ribbon of sky. Samuele peered at its changing light high above him. He did not know why he had made that leap, why he had obeyed the call of the night. Barefoot he had made his way through thorny thickets, over spiky rocks. Then a pitchy nothingness had swallowed him up. Just as a lamb that has made a false step in its blind meanderings suddenly feels emptiness beneath its feet. Plummeting down had been quite the opposite of what he had imagined: instead of falling it had felt like rising up. He had felt the rock surface almost brushing his cheek and had stretched out his arms as if pretending to fly. It was terrifying, but wonderful.

"The earth opened up and I must have fallen, after that I don't remember anything. I didn't hear any voices, though they tell me that the whole village was out looking for me, but it could have been that I fell asleep. I was seven or eight at the time, perhaps, and I hadn't had an easy night of it. My father and mother had had words because we had got back late, and then there was the matter of Boi, who had refused to give us a drink of water. A truly horrible night, as dark as dark can be. And then I jumped off the windowsill and took a step. All I could see was darkness, but I wasn't scared at all. I went on, not thinking of going anywhere, like a dog that takes a sniff and follows its nose: it was the smell of the night. Which is cold and tastes of steel."

He had once put the blade of a knife on his tongue and

had realised that what he sensed was not a taste, but a smell. The smell of the night, in fact. Maybe that was what misled him, the lure of something familiar. So he headed out into the country. Certainly, that night had a smell to it that was like the taste of his knife. Inside that darkness there loomed the trees and the dry, frozen underbrush rustled. The ground beneath his bare feet crackled like *carasau* bread.

Samuele could not have said how far he walked; only that dawn crept up behind the ridge just as he looked skywards to follow the shrieks and curses of a kite.

"I don't know how it was I fell. And I really don't know when I stopped falling. All I know is that falling slowly into that gorge was like drowning in air. And then I stopped. My fall was broken by a juniper bush growing out of a crack. My wrist was hurting, but I could move my legs and head. The depth below me seemed bottomless. Above me, just a narrow ribbon of sky. How long did I hang there looking up at it? How long?

"When the stag peered over the brink the dimness was overcoming me again, but maybe I was nodding off, worn out by fright, but I knew from the antlers that it must be a stag. It craned over the chasm to look at me, but then a clap of thunder scared it away. A fox peered down at me too. The skies were thrashing their whole range of percussion . . . A troop of clouds was marching forwards and thunderclaps barked out the order to attack . . . There, above the ribbon of sky, a battle was raging. It started when the stag looked down at me. Then it was the fox, and after that a boar who wanted to know the how and the why of it, and after them came a sheep and a goat, eager to give me some advice.

"High above they were fighting tooth and nail . . . The hoofs of a wild ass and the claws of a roving cat dislodged small stones like grains of salt that rained down onto me."

*

Up above, for a day and a night, they had been interrogating even the trees and the rocks in search of Samuele. As he walked, Totore Cambosu, his shotgun over his shoulder, told that not long ago Tziu Antoni Palimodde's little daughter had gone missing too . . . Mariangela, she was called. Had they heard about it? And the other men said, yes, they'd heard, even if they hadn't taken part in the search. There's something sinister going on, said the men as the countryside swallowed them up.

As you reach the foot of the mountain the rock begins to crack, the arbutus bushes grow in the crevices and then spread out, calmly taking up residence over the centuries. Those growing in the crevices bear the same berries some Roman legionary might have chewed on to assuage the pangs of hunger when he was lost in that desolate nothingness.

In a word, Mariangela Palimodde had gone missing in those parts not even a month before, but they had already given up looking for her.

By the second night the boar and the wild cats and all the other visions had ceased to visit him. Hanging in the abyss all Samuele could see were the cliff edges that, twenty or thirty metres above, let daylight and darkness pass, then a shaft of sunlight, then a murmur of wind that stirred the dust, then blackness that is the depth of nothingness, traversed by thousands of stars. And Samuele hanging in the abyss, clinging to a juniper, maddened by a loneliness which now gripped him hard and would not let him go.

On the third night what he thought he saw was a swollen moon that tried to reach him halfway down the abyss. A shameless moon too large to enter that gorge . . .

Maybe Samuele thought that weeping might mean that he really was still alive . . . Hunger gnawed at his innards, it was worse than the thirst. So his weeping was like that moon, swollen, enormous. And he almost seemed to feel better, until

51

he heard a voice. But it was not a voice, it was the weeping of another. Against the moonlight he saw a wraithlike shadow, almost transparent.

"Hey!" called the shadow . . . Samuele did not answer. He closed his eyes. His wrist was hurting. "Hey!" the voice repeated. "Hey!"

When he opened his mouth Samuele realised that his lips were parched, glued together, and the only reply he could give was to try to make some gesture with his hand.

The shadow above him appeared to see him perfectly well, with that moonlight behind it that poured like milk into the crevasse. And it spoke with the voice of a little girl . . . And said this wasn't the time to die, that she had thought of it too, when in the thick of the forest no-one had responded to her weeping, but here she was now to respond to his. To tell him about the moon which had led her to the edge of the abyss and had shown him there clinging to the juniper . . . Or so in his delirium Samuele thought the shadow said.

In fact the girl-shadow voice said: "Wake up!"

Sergeant Palmas spread his arms, then tapped his chest a few times.

"Well, strike me dead!" He said this under his breath because you never know who you're dealing with. "Stocchino . . . for the love of God . . ." He called him by his surname as if he really ought to give him a ticking off, whereas he only wanted to say he was glad they had found him, and alive. Perhaps it was relief because there in the woodland he had felt helpless and exposed, and that discovery at least meant that the search was over. Perhaps it was relief because his son Francesco was the same age as Samuele Stocchino, now found miraculously saved by a bush that had broken his fall. Behind him Totore Cambosu was telling about the time Gigetto Aranzolu had been for seven days in the Gurturja cave, sucking water out of the rock wall to keep himself alive. However, the conclusion was that despite what they said in the village, Samuele Stocchino's hour had not yet come and nor had it come for Mariangela Palimodde, who had heard him crying and then had heard voices. That girl had been a miracle, lost for a month in the woods and still alive. So the boy owed his life to the girl, but she owed hers to him as well, because the voices she had heard were those of the men out searching for Samuele.

So they got ropes ready to hoist him out of the abyss. When he felt himself being tied Samuel did not really understand who was shaking him out of his drowsiness. It was a tiny fellow, a lance-corporal from northern Italy who was at home in the mountains . . .

The girl-shadow voice repeated: "Wake up!"

In the village there was a ceaseless bustle: they had gone searching for one and had found two. One saved by a juniper, the other by genetics, because females are survivors born. Precisely what had happened no-one knew. But how it had happened was another story: Mariangela, already dead of cold and exhaustion, had been reprieved by a Saint Anne touched by Samuele's tears. Samuele calling and Mariangela hearing, both of them too young to die.

Antioca planted a nail in her heart and said not a word, for she knew it was no miracle; she knew that Samuele had to go on living to humiliate her, to make her touch the very depths of suffering. She drew her shawl around her shoulders and ran to where they had found him. It was not far, just a step. But no-one knew of that abyss, no-one had ever seen it. So perhaps it had opened up that very night under Samuele's feet. And what about the girl who found him? Perhaps she had got lost for the sole purpose of finding him. Antioca joined the men:

53

the sergeant, that wisp of an Alpine lance-corporal, Totore Cambosu, Felice . . . and all the rest of them.

When Samuele came up on the rope it looked as if the rock had given birth to him. He was red all over, his lips gummed together and a vacant look in his eyes. Then they laid him on the ground. He began to shudder – so at least he was alive. Antioca did not move from where she stood. She looked at Mariangela, whom no-one had come to reclaim, and put her arms around her.

Once home that night Samuele was put to bed. "Incredibly enough he's well," said Dr Milone. "Good constitution," he said. And under his breath, "Incredible . . ." And he gave a great smile.

But Antioca was far from smiling.

"What's up with you?" Felice asked.

"Don't you understand?" she answered.

Felice shook his head. And he was not lying. But what could Antioca say to that dim-witted fellow she had married? How do you go about explaining what is so dazzlingly obvious? So Antioca got out of the bed she shared with her husband and the newborn twins and went to see Samuele, left on his own in the warmth of the kitchen. "Not sleeping?" she asked.

Samuele did not stir, but it was obvious he wasn't asleep. Antioca drew a chair up to the bed and sat down, just as she used to spend her nights by her mother's deathbed. Samuele's eyes were shut tight, but he was not asleep. Antioca leaned close to hear if he was breathing, as she had always done with her children and even with her husband from time to time.

"How long have I been dreaming?" asked Samuele suddenly, as if in his sleep.

"Who are you?" whispered Antioca, her lips almost brushing his.

PART TWO

Much Like a Pain

It was His hand that bore me safely above
the flood . . .

As I Lay Dying, William Faulkner

First Coryphaeus

Spectators or readers as you may be . . . In the theatre of man there are roles assigned. Leading and secondary players take their parts in the ritual of death, the only ritual that speaks of life. The combatant, whether of wars or of existence, is formed in the bed of the dear departed and the women "read life" to him. Intrinsic to the role-playing game of giving birth, nursing and loving are the power to reject death and the humility to accept it. The mother of all mourners blends together sorrow and contentment: sorrow for a life that has ended, contentment for a journey that has reached its due conclusion. A son, a brother, a husband inert on his deathbed, they are still alive in the words: "that's what he was, he did that, how handsome he was, how brave". A life is a perpetual fire of memories and the soul a burning ember under the ashes. The mother of all mourners takes pride in this knowledge, as if it were a goal achieved.

"*A mie toccat su piantu, / a mie su sentimentu.*"

She must weep because the deceased is hers, because in this new affliction there is only the one hope, that of cheating death. The mother of all mourners has to face the problem that afflicts her: daughter of her father, mother of her son, wife to her husband, yet mother to her father, wife to her son, daughter to her son. "*A chie mi lassas fizzu / a chie, babbu amorosu, / a chie divinu isposu . . .*"

In the theatre of man there are metres assigned. The stubborn persistence of the septenarius in six-line stanzas. The lament that casts a spell on the tragedy, the deception that approaches as it departs. The solitude of One that is All solitudes. Other mothers, other sisters, other wives will be thrust to the centre of the stage by angels of annunciation, trembling bearers of sorrow.

Here the scene is in progress, we take it from the centre, from the heart of the action, which is not action but only the account of action. There is the dead man, there is the mother, daughter, wife, sister, and there is Death silently looking on, refusing to give explanations but also taking part.

They are seated together, Death and the mother of all mourners, and they embrace each other, weeping.

I

Benghazi and back

"Stocchino Samuele, aged eighteen, shepherd, single, despite having attended primary school only until the second year is able to read and write sufficiently well.

"He is of slender build, but very strong; height 1.63 m with a long armspan of 1.67 m. Maximum skull circumference of 542 mm; the frontal curve being 280 mm, the rear 260 mm; the right and left lateral measurements 270 mm respectively; the longitudinal curve 330, the biauricular 340; the anteroposterior diameter 190; probable average cranial capacity 1537. Cephalic index 71.1; skull type: dolichocephalic.

"Frontal sinuses and eyebrow arch perfectly regular; the forehead is average, smooth, not covered by the hair; the face is round, effeminate; the eye is long and very bright; the nose short and straight; the upper canines are very long; there are no large gaps between the upper incisors; the lips are moist; the lower jaw is bulky; the hair is thick, smooth, tawny in colour; the complexion is rosy.

"The pupilary reflexes are instant. The strength of grip is considerable, the dynamometer shows thirty-eight for the pressure of the right hand and thirty-one for the left. The pulse rate is sixty-five beats per minute, in which time the breath was drawn twenty-three times. The temperature in the armpit is 36.9°.

"When naked he appears well built, with a sinewy torso, narrow hips and buttocks; fully developed testicles, average penis; pubic hair scanty.

"Tapering hands and feet.

"The subject appears reasonably intelligent and gives ready, decisive answers; asked why he wished to enter the Royal Army as a volunteer he replied that he wishes to serve his country. Asked which country he wished to serve, after a noticeable pause he carefully pronounced: It-a-ly.

"He is declared fit for service."

Sometimes he could imagine his death. It was like a thought hardening into reality. The ultimate fear becoming so familiar as to cease to be fear any more. He could feel the pitching of the ferry at the mercy of the waves. It was like simultaneously seeing the end of life and its beginning. His young warrior heart, along with another thousand or more, had been swallowed up by the steel belly of a ship and now was learning the power of the sea in storm. It was an unrelenting, unending, abominable intermingling of flesh and bodies and breath. This was the sea, this was the horror that surrounded his homeland. Now that land was more distant than ever, but being distant did not mean that it was anywhere. The sea was a nothingness. This he remembered.

Only forty-eight hours before – a whole lifetime – the port of Brindisi had been a swaying forest of masts, a hundred or more invincible ships with the cross of Christ and the Savoia coat of arms emblazoned on their hulls and the might of thousands of gun-barrels. A force at the service of the Faith and of Progress against the Turkish foe.

With all the zeal of his sixteen years Samuele Stocchino from Arzana, *soi-disant* eighteen-year-old, fit for service and enrolled, had fallen to his knees and kissed the grey paving of the quayside, praying to fate that his first expedition might take him straight to the ranks of the heroes. With a hand trembling not with fear but with emotion, he had delivered the documents authorising him to embark, along with his unknown comrades of the Fourth Infantry Regiment. But as he boarded the vessel he had had a dizzy spell, because at that moment his destiny was decided. His body had become the puppet of a frenzy that sparkled in his eyes. And the same identical look could be seen in the faces of thousands of men crowded on the quay, waiting to be swallowed up by the yawning jaws of the ships. A convoy of nine troopships escorted by the battleships *Regina Elena*, *Roma* and *Napoli*, the dreadnought *Amalfi*, the cruisers *Piemonte*, *Liguria*, *Etruria* and *Lombardia*, and a squadron of destroyers and torpedo boats, protected by that queen of vessels, the flagship *Vittorio Emanuele*. A whole fleet in readiness to sail to Benghazi. To Benghazi which, thought Samuele, was nothing but an island just like the one he had left behind him. Then someone told him he was an ignorant nitwit, that it was not only islands that floated on the infinite sea, but also peninsulas and continents. But how was it possible to contradict him? You could not call Samuele Stocchino an ignorant nitwit; not down there in the icy belly of a troopship:

"Nobody calls *me* an ignorant nitwit!" he had hissed.

Maybe that had been the first – and the longest – sentence he had ever uttered in Italian . . . *Fizzu 'e bagassa!* he muttered to himself in Sardinian.

Word had it that the flagship was quite something. Like a palace, it would take a whole lifetime to see round, they said. The living quarters were a luxurious royal palace panelled with precious woods.

After seven hours at sea with a favourable wind the flagship reached the western coast of Greece, the troopships, battle-ships, destroyers and torpedo boats all following like a row of ducklings.

"Where are we? Where are we?" a dry-lipped youngster kept on asking.

"Cyprus," someone said.

"Cyprus? Like hell it's Cyprus . . . We're level with Crete, you duffers . . . In the middle, between the islands of Malta and Crete, to be exact," put in a sailor who was bringing them something to drink.

What difference did that make? One island after another. I'm right, thought Samuele, locked in a stubborn silence. Outside my own country there are only islands. Sardinias everywhere, thought Samuele; Sardinias scattered over the oceans, thrown at random into the seas. At Cyprus, Rhodes, Crete, Malta and who knows where else . . . ?

The storm broke just offshore from the port of Benghazi. A ferocious storm. Driving rain, salt, iron and night. The ship bent and hissed like a whale. At one moment it seemed to be lying on its side, the next it was upright again. And so on, time without end.

Samuele Stoccino's entry into the field of human conflict was baptised by a north-easter that battered at the bows and torrential rain that made the decks cry out.

In the foaming din of the sea and the wind the yells of the recruits were like the whispers of the dying. The song of the waves brought with it the fearful certainty that no safe place was safe, either in the ship of out of it.

Then a sudden dead calm halted the entire fleet. Prisoners of nothingness now. Just as they had been hurled into an infernal stretch of sea, now it seemed that safety must be in sight. On the motionless surface they could see slivers of land. They were islands too.

"Where are we?"

"At Benghazi, at Benghazi, idiot!"

The flagship hoisted the battle colours . . .

But it was only a temporary lull. Within the hour, just as landing operations began, the sea began to seethe even more violently than before.

It had been like death. Except that he could remember it.

When his bunk started to rock so much that he had to cling to the sides so as not to be thrown out of it. And his head was slimy with vomit.

Thus it was that Samuele Stocchino opened his eyes and for a moment still felt unsteady. Until the certainty of the light of dawn put a stop to the swaying.

Slipping his legs from under the blankets, he sat on the side of the bed and tried to focus on the small area lit by the faint glow of the embers in the fireplace. He planted his bare feet on the cold floor to make sure it was solid.

. . . *No sooner were the battle colours hoisted than the ships opened fire on Giuliana beach, where the infantry were due to land. The warships targeted Berka barracks and the castle, over which the Turkish flag was flying: it was felled by the first salvo.*

At 8.50 hours, under covering fire from the ships and led by Captain Frank, despite beating rain and a rough sea, the landing parties disembarked with a few 76 calibre guns and positioned themselves on the crest of the dunes, with the artillery on their left, so as to enable the sappers to build a few pontoons over which the troops began to flow . . .

And after that? What else did Samuele have to tell about the outside world? What did he say about Tripolitania? And about the landing in Cirenaica? About that parched and barren land that cost so many lives he scarcely knew what to say. Felice urged him, because he had always liked soldiers' tales. But Samuele didn't know what to say about soldiers; all he remembered was the forced marches in the broiling sun and the multiple scaffolds for hanging Bedouin. So he told of the first time he sank a bayonet into a human body . . .

At 15.30 hours the Fourth Infantry began a manoeuvre, advancing in two ranks some distance apart in non-vulnerable formation and perfect order. Seen from the beach and the ships, that advance over open ground up a gentle slope and under enemy fire appeared a truly admirable application of the soundest tactical criteria, and could be carried out with increasing efficiency throughout its whole course. The brigadier had ordered the troops, already exhausted by the efforts of the morning, to ground their packs. With perfect timing General Ameglio in person led the frontal attack by the sailors and a mixed battalion of the Fourth and Sixty-Third Infantry.

Between Sibbah and the salt lake they sent us, two platoons of the Fourth and a company and a half of the Sixty-Third, to cover the sailors protecting the landing troops. Bullets were flying everywhere . . . That area is dry and uneven, and the Bedouin were like louse eggs in your hair . . . There was nothing for it but to rout them out and prevent them from shooting at the sappers building the pontoons. I don't even remember how I got off the ship, I can't even tell you that. In that rough sea Saint Christopher came to help us and carried us on his shoulders. Well, anyway, drenched, *iffustu che unu puzoneddu*, I found myself on the beach. Always on the waves, though . . . No change. At our backs the billows of the sea, before us billows of red earth swimming with Bedouin, they too as red as the earth. And they were firing. There were thirty of us in a hollow and as soon as we stuck a head up there was trouble. Those devils howled like mad beasts, like rabid dogs, seeing the Italian troops, once off the ships, beginning to crawl across the sand like so many black crabs. So the Bedouin howled, as if to say that either we shoot or we die, and when the ammunition runs out either we kill or we die. I understood this as if I'd always known it. Down in that hollow it seemed as if we'd been buried alive, we began to think we'd better get out of there . . . Who was the highest in rank? Who the hell was? There was no-one of higher rank in there . . . Only the vultures waiting for us. One fellow who tried to escape

64

got a bullet between the eyes; another got one in the back. There was no way we could see out to get in a shot, those devils just kept on firing and firing . . .

But it was difficult to dislodge the Arabs from the trenches. The two senior officers present, Commander Frank and Lieutenant-Colonel Gangitano, both suffered very serious wounds, as did two company commanders and other officers. General Ameglio thereupon took up position in the front line and led the troops in a series of bayonet attacks which soon assured possession of the trenches. Meanwhile the sun was sinking fast and the remainder of the operation was carried out in semi-darkness.

"And then?" asked Felice, spellbound.

"And then the only thing was to invoke some saint, for there was barely a chance of getting out of there alive . . . I said that we should do what they don't expect. To leave here, I said, is to walk straight into the lion's mouth. And what's more, I can't bear to be in a rat's hole. But who's going to kill me, eh? Tell me that! Wait for darkness, I said. If we can't see them, they can't see us . . . So I got out into the open with the bullets whistling around my ears. Pitch blackness all around, just some lights down at the beach and the flashes from the ships' guns. The sea was now calm. It was a starry night, but there was no moon. While I was running for the beach I heard heavy breathing close behind me. Who knows how many of us had managed to escape from the hollow . . . ? Of course, you don't realise these things while you're fighting, do you? . . . I was running and a Bedouin as black as the devil, or rather as red, was there right before my eyes, so close we could have been chatting. I made as if to shake him by the hand, but my hand was a bayonet. His eyes widened till the whites showed and he almost embraced me

"The steel pierced the Bedouin's chest as a spit pierces

a lamb. With a sound of something soft yet tough, the skin beneath the outer skin. The layer that covers the muscles . . . That's what puts up a resistance and makes a noise when it's torn. Because a wound is like a mouth sucking in steel, it relishes the savour of it, it drinks in all the taste of the blade. The taste that, as I know well, is night . . ."

But the taste of night is something Samuele cannot explain: it is a feeling without an explanation. Hence it was that in the childlike mind of Felice, lapping up war stories, that tale ended with the Bedouin and Private Samuele Stocchino embracing each other in the night-time.

Therefore that thought was, as it were, trapped between brain and breast, paralysed by the lack of language. But it was throbbing all the same. As embarrassing as not finding the name for a thing. Embarrassment, another word which came to mind before being really born. Embarrassment was an arrhythmia of the breath, it was like . . . It was like that return from the christening party ten years ago, or when he had been engulfed by the night and ended up in the abyss. Like when he had decided to enrol for Libya . . .

There was certainly a funny side to it.

"I'm tired now," he said softly, with the ghost of a smile.

Felice stared at him and then, understanding at last, nodded to himself and left the room.

On 24 February, 1912, during the crossing from Benghazi to Tripoli, Private Samuele Stocchino began to spit blood.

He was a little local hero: as a marksman he was not up to much, but in hand-to-hand fighting he was unrivalled. He threw himself at the enemy as if he wished to embrace him, made a man's war by acting like a woman on heat. He flattered and charmed his adversary, promised him kisses and caresses, and then raped him with a bayonet. And the other was almost happy to abandon himself to the good death bestowed on him by the steel. As the faithful slave would steady the sword onto which the noble suicide was to fall, so he, simply and lovingly, dispensed their end.

Ah, if all his victims had been able to speak, if we had been able to question the lifeless bodies and they had been permitted to answer, those Bedouin corpses, fists pressed to their breast to embrace the blade, would have said with what gentle languor they had thrown themselves to the wild beast, with what feathery lightness they had fallen before they tasted the scorching sand. And with what loving look, what sweetest sweetness, what exquisite deliciousness, they had given themselves to be run through.

He was a little local hero, the only one of the troop who had no complaints about helping the medical officer to confirm the death of men they had hanged. Sometimes even the M.O. had had enough of Bedouin corpses left to dry under the blazing sun, but not he. He did his duty meticulously: check the pulse, hold a mirror to the nostrils.

He was a mere foot soldier who had found a meaning in life. He did not stand out in a crowd, he was simply an enterprising butcher's boy in the Award-winning Italian Butchery. He was the agent on earth of Death & Co. Now there was something he knew, but had no name for. The wolf pulsing in his heart had grown its fangs.

II

Looking for one thing you find another:
recounting the time when Samuele lost his virginity

If Felice liked war stories, Gonario liked stories about women. This elder brother had become rough and hairy, the very picture of a shepherd. But he had remained a hireling. Now he had a few sheep of his own that he could graze along with his masters'. At twenty he had lost his virginity with a travelling prostitute. And now there he was wanting to hear about all the black girls who've had it wet and warm ever since they were children.

Samuele gave a shrug. He had seen them, both consenting and otherwise. He had seen those who sought out a white body as if it were a rare jewel, and those who rejected it as something disgusting. He had seen whole platoons raping old women with shrivelled dugs, and even little boys. Gonario urged him on:

"And what about you, eh? I can just imagine you . . ." And he smiled that smile of his, lowering his head so as not to show his bad teeth. Even now as a grown man Gonario was still as shy and bashful as a child.

"The women there are like they are here," said Samuele shortly.

And this was an answer that had Gonario blushing to the roots of his hair.

As for Samuele, he had liked killing more than fucking. But one cannot say such things, so he confined himself, without going into detail, to telling of the time he had enjoyed himself with the daughter of a chieftain. What he did not mention was that Corporal Políto was also present.

Políto was nineteen, the son of a bigshot in the army, a very big one, in fact nothing short of a lieutenant-general, so they said. But he was a hothead. The story had it that this bigshot father had refused to make things easy for him. And that his elder brother was about to be made Ambassador to Egypt. And that his younger sister was about to marry a certain Count Pallavicini. But nothing of this nobility could be discerned in the face of Saverio Políto. He ought to have been punished. He *ought* to have been. Oh yes, he was a real hothead – Lieutenant Marchioro got goose pimples if he saw him anywhere near . . . He was as long and lean as a Gothic Christ figure. He was pursued by barrack-room gossip like a fox by a pack of hounds. Was he the illegitimate son of his brass-braided father and a serving wench? Had he begun to shave at the age of ten? Did he have the biggest cock in the whole army? Had he, as a mere stripling, been the lover of Eleonora Duse?

Be that as it may, Lieutenant Marchioro sent for Samuele. He arrived, saluted, clicked his heels, said, "Yes, sir?" and all that. The officer, who was prodding away at a dental abscess, did not so much as turn round . . .

It was 10 p.m., with a muggy heat that stuck to your back. Marchioro had received him in his private room, which was a bare little cubicle not unlike a cemetery chapel: just enough room for the pallet, a chest of drawers, a washbasin. No, it was not up to much, but all the same a step up from sleeping in the barrack hut with forty or fifty others, or in tents where the wild beasts of the night did not recognise a strip of canvas as a barrier . . . Marchioro, wearing the expression of a proto-Christian martyr, arranged a heavy woollen sweater on the chair beside his bed.

"It'll soon get chilly," he said, almost to himself. Samuele stiffened, and sharpened up his military salute. "At ease, Stocchino, at ease . . . Do you realise why I've sent for you?"

Samuele did not answer, as he knew perfectly well that whatever the lieutenant had to say he would say anyway.

Eventually he said, "Políto", and that was enough. Samuele gave a nod. Políto, of course. The lieutenant added, "At the Black Dragon."

Samuele saluted again, his elbow quivering, like a young actor leaving the stage. The breeze from the half-open door told him it was indeed beginning to cool off.

No-one ever laid a finger on Políto, however much they said to the contrary. He did what he wanted, and up at H.Q. they simply did not want to hear about it. In this case, for example, it was a good two kilometres from the camp to Barce. And he had to make his way there discreetly and get the fellow out of the brothel.

The Black Dragon was a joint where the lads would risk losing their cigarette money and even their leave, and sometimes they risked their health into the bargain. The girls they could afford were not always "clean". At twenty some of them already looked ancient: withered, toothless, flattened dugs, skeletal faces . . . But Políto knew how to pick and choose, and for him even at fifteen they were already too old.

When Samuele entered the room he had been directed to, Políto was busy at work on a little black girl who screamed at every thrust. The sight was an indescribable combination of incongruous bodies: Políto's hairy arse and muscled thighs, and the dark ankles and rose-pink soles of the feet of the child. Make no mistake about it, she was still a child. Samuele rattled the door with his heel to warn the corporal of his presence. Políto heard him but did not turn, did not stop; in fact he thrust even more violently and the girl gave voice even louder. When he eventually left off and withdrew from the girl Samuele had plenty of time to ascertain the truth about Políto's legendary member. He should, of course, have been embarrassed, but in the course of verifying deaths with the M.O. he had seen everything. He had seen things that had escaped from living beings who had died before they could become aware of having done them: hanged men who had shat in their pants, who had blasted out vomit as soon as the noose was loosened, strung-up corpses that pissed and farted. And erections under their robes . . .

So it was that seeing the corporal naked, sweating and with cock erect, it seemed to him almost like a living version of the death he had learned to have dealings with.

Políto knew all this very well. He was one of those who always seem on the point of committing suicide, but for some unknown reason change their mind and persuade themselves that either they are immortal or that it's up to someone else to kill them. Maybe it would be gonorrhoea, or malaria, or yellow fever. Or else a husband whose wife he'd had, or a woman he had left in the lurch. Or a son of his he refused to recognise – but there was time enough for that. This corporal, in all his twenty years of life, had done nothing but sow the seeds of his own death, like scattering breadcrumbs in a wood. In any case, whether he had finished or not, Políto grabbed hold of his trousers and pulled them up to cover his erection . . . At which point the girl flew off the handle.

"Haven't you had enough yet?" Políto teased the child, but she reached out to him, grasped him around the waist and fumbled at his flies . . . "That's enough, I have to go now," he said with a glance at Samuele. But the girl did not give up. Without a word Samuele made for the door but: "Stocchino!" Samuele froze. "Do you know how to use this bayonet as well?" he asked, pointing to his crotch. Samuele did not answer. Políto had meanwhile almost finished buttoning up his shirt. "Come

71

here," he said, and it sounded like an order. Samuele paused a moment, then moved towards the bed. Políto gave the child a smile. She smiled back. The corporal motioned the private to come a little closer, and he smelled of night, and steel, and blood; then he grabbed Samuele by the belt. "It's already paid for," he said. "I'll go and have a drink, then we'll be on our way back. No hurry."

Without waiting for an answer out he went, still tucking in his shirt tails . . .

"An African whore," remarked Gonario, who had not lost a single word of the story and was now purple in the face.

Samuele burst out laughing and had a fit of coughing in the process. "Help me up," he said.

Gonario picked him up as if he were a child. He was a burly fellow, and his life in the open air had made him tanned and sinewy. He sat him upright on the side of the bed and little by little the cough subsided. Samuele could breathe again.

"What then?" asked Gonario when his brother had recovered his breath.

"How d'you mean, what then?" taunted Samuele.

"Well, you know . . ."

"What do you want to know?" said Samuele, playing cat and mouse.

"Oh, nothing . . . just that . . ." Gonario played for time: "This African tart was paid for, wasn't she?"

"Políto left me alone with the girl and you can imagine the rest," concluded Samuele.

But on the contrary, he didn't imagine it, he didn't imagine it at all . . .

Since being invalided home Samuele had seemed almost sensible. Africa had made a man of him; despite the pneumonia that had

72

greatly weakened him, he now walked upright and was sure of himself. All those parts of him that had been merely sketched in, almost without outline, now looked perfectly designed: his neckline, for example, or the tendons of his wrist. To Gonario, at times, he did not even seem to be his brother. Whenever Doctor Milone made him pull up his shirt to examine his chest, Gonario always thought that he looked thinner with his clothes on . . .

What was scary about Samuele was that time and again he got to the brink of death, and then not even death really wanted him and sent him back.

Alone with the girl in that room in the brothel, Samuele's first thought was of flight. There on the bed she was reciting a whole liturgy of blandishments, but he was still on his feet and saw only himself.

"What's your name?" he asked hoarsely.

"Teresa," she said, pronouncing every syllable of that incongruous name with the accuracy of one who has studied the answer meticulously.

"How old are you?" whispered Samuele.

The little girl gave him a questioning look: "Don't you fancy me?" she asked. "It's all paid for," she urged, opening her legs a little. To Samuele the room smelled of bad meat. Night had knifed down like a guillotine and it was beginning to get chilly. Samuele shuddered, looked at the girl again and gave a great gulp. "You shy," she said. "You no here other time." Samuele nodded: perfectly right, I've never been here before. "Yes?" she said, misunderstanding the gesture.

"No, no," said Samuele.

"Come here," urged Teresa.

And Samuele saw himself when, in the pitchy black of the ambush, bayonet in hand, he had made that identical enticement to the Bedouin, or to the perfidious Turk: "Come here to me" . . . And come they had.

So he took a step forward . . .

"You shy of it," murmured Teresa as she undid his flies. Then, pulling out his penis, like a third-rate actress she scolded him for having hesitated: "You no shame. My gentleman have no shame."

Samuele was still standing. Teresa slid him into her mouth . . .

Experiencing something for the very first time can mean not recognising oneself. Now, while his body reasoned and reacted independently from him, Samuele seemed to be seeing himself from the lip of the abyss, as had the stag and the other animals. Now it was he who was peering over the rim of the rock, seeing himself clinging to the juniper tree twenty or thirty metres below.

And still he did not recognise himself, but he perfectly remembered the langour of that fall. Indeed that languor was one with the violent pulsing that now shook his breast.

Teresa took him by the hips and urged him towards her. She was eating him, surely, she was eating him alive and he, a throbbing foodstuff, was discovering the impassioned generosity of becoming a comestible. A moment later he no longer needed guiding. You could say anything of Samuele, except that he wasn't a fast learner . . .

III

Big-game hunting

The news from Tripoli was far from good. Allies had turned
into enemies, sheep had turned into wolves. While they were
certifying the deaths of six rebels, the M.O. told Samuele that
where they were stationed, towards Benghazi, it was practically
a holiday. Albeit a holiday of daily sorties, little attacks from
the desert, of oases as dangerous as mousetraps are for mice, of
infected water and deadly insects. But still a holiday, because in
Tripoli there had been an uprising. At first they had pretended
to welcome the Italians as saviours, but they "had not kept
their word". That was how they put it in the dormitory. But
Puddu from Oliena, who had studied in Rome, said that it wasn't
really treachery to fight for your own country.

"Ah, by God, they're not all blockheads like Sardinians,
eh?" It was not nice to hear it said, but there was a certain truth
in it. "All the same," he went on, "who the hell ever said we had
become Italians?"

"A fine thing," agreed Mariani from Orune, "us being
watchdogs in a foreign country after giving away our own."

But to Samuele this sort of talk seemed to make no sense.
Not because he did not understand his mates – and when it
came down to it he agreed with them – but because for him
things were simply the way they were: you may think you can
interfere with them or control them, but you can't. This is
ageless wisdom, part of what you know without knowing why
you know it. And what was as clear as daylight, even in Benghazi,

was that wherever you turned you would see or hear a Sardinian. And that those Sardinians, including himself, had no earthly reason for being there.

"Not to mention the fact," insisted Puddu, "that they treated us just like they're telling us to treat the Turks. In fact they treated us worse."

At this point Samuele shut him up, because he knew you can find yourself on the brink of a precipice where it's only a small step between saying what comes out of your mouth and ending up against a wall facing a firing squad.

"Shut up!" he said. "Shut your gob."

Because even when you're in the right, you have to find the right time and place to have your say, don't you? Isn't that so? Learning that there are rules is the best way not of obeying but of disobeying. And he, Samuele, was fed up to the gills with hearing theories about what is right and what is wrong. They were all excellent fellows, for goodness' sake, but they had not realised that the masters become masters precisely because they have rules, they even make them themselves, whereas those who sit there grouching about this and that will never become masters, they will be nothing but hirelings for ever and a day, because the only rules they like are the ones that other people have to follow.

"Outside Sardinia we are all Sardinians," murmured Samuele, unable to restrain himself. "But when we're there, at home, it's each man for himself."

Puddu from Oliena was forced to admit as much, but he yielded the point as if he did not really agree at all. In fact he went straight on to say that it was right, it was sacrosanct, to oppose the laws and regulations of tyrants. To declare that the self-determination of a people and all that . . . Samuele was not even listening, Mariani from Orune nodded along, but you could see his thoughts were miles away.

76

"So why did you join up for this war?" Samuele demanded point blank.

Puddu stopped abruptly and looked him in the eye. "Friend . . ." he began.

"I'm not your friend. What's this, are we all friends now? Go on, tell me: *A itte bi ses benniu in gherra?*"

Puddu's face darkened: "*Ca m'ana custrintu,*" he said curtly.

"That's just what I wanted to say: if you're your own master, there's no-one who can force you . . ."

"And what about you?" put in Mariani.

"I came because I decided to. *Pro contu meu, ca deo so su mere meu,*" snapped Samuele.

In any case, the Arabs who should have been grateful to their Italian saviours kept attacking from the oases, from the lines between Bu Meliana and Gargaresh, while the Turks attacked from the sea. The Bersaglieri of the Eleventh Brigade were literally between the devil and the deep blue sea, it was said. But even in Tripoli itself, without the least warning, they began firing at Italian soldiers from the houses and alleyways. That explained it all, and showed the discrepancy between theory and practice.

Lieutenant Marchioro gave a shrug: "Now we'll see," he said. No-one made a comment. It was evident that Marchioro was a soldier by vocation, as a doctor or a priest has to be. "Now we'll see," he repeated.

The dispatches from Tripoli brought terrible news. Eighty Bersaglieri of the Eleventh had been besieged in a cemetery in the village of Henni, and forty of them had been captured by the Arabs and Turks.

"The young Bersaglieri who died on 23 October did not die merely as heroes, but also as martyrs," read Marchioro, his voice breaking with emotion.

Clearly he had become a soldier because he believed that there must be some region, some battlefield, in which man fought for the whole of his civilisation. But in Tripoli he had realised that a people must be allowed the right to choose even their own oppressor. What was that baker's son doing at Henni, the one they had crucified, castrated and mutilated? What was he doing there, eh?

The M.O. urged him to lower his voice: "You're exhausted and this climate is weakening you," he diagnosed. Marchioro nodded.

"Now we'll see," he repeated in an almost imperceptible whisper. Not a word more.

And see they did: the machinery of repression marched swiftly on. These Italians were fine fellows, no doubt about that, but it did not do to rouse them to anger. They were turning Tripoli inside out, like a sock. "There'd be plenty for you to do there," Políto told Samuele one day. "Counting up the dead," he added for the sake of clarity.

In the open spaces of the quarters of the city razed to the ground by artillery and machine-gun fire, they had planted forests of scaffolds: the women and children were beneath the rubble, the grown men and boys were swinging in the wind. Those who had been there said that the stench of death was so strong that people went around with face masks anywhere within twenty kilometres of Tripoli. All this seemed quite understandable to Samuele, who even thought he could smell the sweetish odour that a hanged man's skin gives off, and it seemed to him that he could say for sure that death is really a very simple thing, like eating and drinking. In his childhood thoughts death was a cruel theft, but then he learned that it can even be a blessing . . . He pictured the death of the crucified Bersagliere, and it was as if death were watching someone's unwished-for life, until she was bid welcome to put an end to so much suffering. So he could easily imagine the smile of that Bersagliere, with such a wealth of youth that he had never thought of wishing to die like that, just to put an end to suffering.

Puddu from Oliena told them about a relation of his who had had a border dispute with a landowner in Mamoiada, and one day they had found him cut in pieces and tied to a tree. The head here and the hands there, one foot still whole while the other must have been eaten by wild boar. And then there was the torso, still tied to the tree. Now, it was clear enough who had committed this outrage, wasn't it? But it was not that simple. They said that there were no certain proofs . . . Until a doctor opened the corpse's mouth and found part of a finger with a ring on it. Twice two is four: they brought in the Mamoiada landowner who, strange to relate, had a bandaged hand because he had lost a finger and, stranger still, it was the very finger they had found in the dead man's mouth. They asked him to show them the wound, but the relations and hired shepherds hastened to swear that he had cut off his finger while chopping wood. So they asked him to show them the finger, but he answered that he had buried it because it wasn't his property but belonged to the Lord. So they showed him the ring and he said, yes, that was his ring, but it had been stolen some time before. So the sergeant who was questioning him told him that none of his answers made sense, that the finger had been found in the dead man's mouth, or more precisely, in the throat of the dismembered body of Eusebio Pillittu, his sworn enemy, and it was his and nobody else's, clear as daylight. So then the landowner told him that as well as the two rivals there was a third person, and he was the one who had bitten off the finger and hidden it in the corpse's mouth. So the sergeant asked him who this third person was, but he refused to name him, said he'd rather go to jail than turn informer. So the

79

sergeant said, very well then, come along to the barracks and we'll see if the missing finger is the same, if the ring was stolen or not, and if there's a third person who's licking his chops. So then the landowner said: Just a moment, to give me time to say goodbye to my wife who is cutting up a pig in the kitchen. And the whole thing happened in a flash. A few moments later, white as a blanched sheet, the Mamoidana landowner gave himself up to the carabinieri. He was the same as before, but lacking one hand . . . It took the sergeant a moment to cotton on to what had happened, but by then it was too late. Pushing everyone aside he rushed into the kitchen where the mistress of the house and her servants were making sausages. The landowner, gripping his stump, collapsed to the ground. The sergeant came back from the kitchen just in time to see him fall. His hand had been severed at the wrist by a blow from a cleaver, but how to prove it? Both flesh and bone had already been minced. Impossible to reconstruct the hand, impossible to prove anything at all . . .

"Take him to hospital in Nuoro," ordered the sergeant. "Otherwise he'll bleed to death."

Puddu stopped there. A few people looked at him questioningly.

"Well, you see," he tried to explain, "who knows if we in this foreign land aren't a bit like that landowner, who risked death rather than admit the wrong he had done . . . ?"

Políto did not know whether to laugh or cry.

Samuele gave him an almost tender look: "Us?" he asked after a while, but it wasn't really a question. "We're like that finger in the mouth," he said.

Políto understood that one.

In any case, orders came for us to be transferred to Tripoli: things were going really badly there. So they told us to embark

at once and that the whole of the Fourth was going there to rein-
force the Fifty-Sixth. The M.O. asked me whether I was feeling
alright. I told him that I did feel a bit tired and then I had this
cough I couldn't get rid of. After that they called me to H.Q.,
where Marchioro handed me an envelope: they had made me a
corporal. Then we had to get our kit ready for the transfer.

Well, then: on 24 February, 1912, during the sea crossing from
Benghazi to the port of Tripoli, the health of Private Samuele
Stocchino, now a corporal, grew worse. He began to spit blood.
Weather conditions were appalling.

It had been like dying. Except that he could remember it.

The crowded troopships had to hug the coast to avoid a
fearful storm out there in the open sea. In his weakened state,
Samuele was gasping for air like a stranded fish. And he
knew what that meant, it was almost like retaliation, because
hundreds of times he had sat there watching the gaping mouths
of fish cast up on the rocks on the river banks. He had looked
at the fish and the fish had looked at him as if begging for
mercy, then flapped about to hurl themselves back into the
water and breathe again . . .

"Don't go anywhere near him!" shouted Políto to make
himself heard above the crashing of the waves against the hull.

Tremendous buffets. But truly terrifying ones. Sudden
squalls, a mass of water piling up against the ship's side. Those
who knew how to pray were saying their prayers and it was at
least seven hours until they were due to reach Tripoli.

Those seven hours became sixteen. The M.O. had ordered
sugar and water to keep Samuele going, but it seemed clear that
he would not make it to Tripoli.

That crossing became a dress rehearsal. He was well aware
that he was on the brink of death. He realised it from the fact
that the ship had suddenly stopped rolling. He was plunged into

a dense slumber, sucking air through a hollow reed as he had done as a boy of thirteen or so when, to scare the women at the wash-trough, he had ducked underwater and tugged at their sheets from the bottom of the trough. He knew he had arrived in the presence of Lady Death because he could see his own self sitting on his bunk . . .

I see myself with blood dribbling from my mouth, take a good look at myself and don't like what I see. Could that heap of bones lying lifeless on the bunk be me? That empty sack thrown hither and thither by the waves? What has become of Corporal Samuele Stocchino?

Back at home they'll be saying: Who knows? Dead there in Libya like the flower of our young men. Congestion of the lungs, ah, the pity of it! And he'd really showed his mettle. No, no, you have to give it to him, that's for sure. Dead at sea, in the dark, poor thing. And what a death, one of those damnable ones, long and drawn out, in sweat and pain and even in delirium. Which he sees in flesh and blood even where it isn't, sitting on his deathbed, just as now. Then he feels he is being borne away somewhere, but not upon the sea: that is where he has left his mortal remains. No, he feels he is being carried to a place near Osini and its name is S'Argiola e' sa Perda, a place among ilex trees. He sees himself being carried there by men in caps, one holding him under the arms and the other two by the ankles: the embrace of the juniper bush. The men are running through the wood and he can feel their panting breath on him, because this rag of a man, bleeding from the mouth and on the verge of death, looked as slender as a reed, but now, carrying him, he is a lot heavier than they thought.

The sky above S'Argiola 'e sa Perda is as blue as Bluebeard's beard or the tunics of the French Hussars, blue as the abyss when it grows dense . . . The blue of the colour in a dream that always sticks in the mind when you've dreamed in colour and what you remember is a terrible colour, brighter than life. That sky is much more than a sky, it is the dream of a sky. It is a cloudless delirium, the ceiling of a country parish church . . .

As they trudge along bearing Samuele's body, the three men in caps find that more and more the earth draws it downwards towards itself. They are wearying, they almost allow the body to brush against the stones, the low shrubs, the nettles, the thistles, the buds. That carting along, that heaving breath, that letting go, that gradual loosening of the elbows and knee joints that eventually forces them just to drag him along . . . Yes, all this Corporal Samuele Stocchino sees of himself as the troopship is fighting to stay afloat in Libyan waters. Even though the captain has chosen to hug the coast . . .

In his mouth abyssal night: rotten blood, iron. Icy tang of inexplicable feelings, falling, rising. Like holding out or giving up . . .

That night Gonario Stocchino had a vision . . . As he was sleeping the gate of the sheepfold burst open and there stood a boy. He was weeping; he said he was lost. Gonario sat up, still dazed with sleep. What do you mean, lost? Who are you, *cuius es?* he asked. "I am Samuele Stocchino de sos de Crabile," said the boy. So Gonario burst out laughing, because he knew that when you have visions those visions are never about things you know, but about mysterious things unknown, things you cannot even speak about. All the same, in his simple heart he realised that the image he had before his eyes could not in any way be his brother, who was far away in Libya fighting the infidels. Nevertheless, in his simple heart he realised that this family mystery might also be a double mystery, or a presentiment, a message of some sort. All this thinking and puzzling confused him a bit, but all the same he told the boy to come in. In he came, and the glow from the embers enabled Gonario to make out his face.

Certainly, thought Gonario, it might be Samuele who from who knows where is trying to tell me something. Nothing wrong with that, is there? Nothing unusual. Blood is thicker than water, after all. So Gonario tells the lad to sit down, stay overnight, we'll sort it all out in the morning. Have you had anything to eat? But the lad does not seem to have any need of that earthly sort, he just seems lost, gazing around him. Gonario is a little unsettled by that heavy silence: he prefers the empty silence of the flocks. So he asks the lad if he is sleepy. The answer is a shake of the head. My brother has the same name as yours, says Gonario, but he's away at war now. The lad nods, he knows that. And he also knows everything that Gonario doesn't know he knows. Is it a vision or not? "I want to tell you that your brother is on the verge, on the very brink between the living and the dead . . ." Gonario seeks for words to answer him, but the youth makes a sign to him to hold his tongue: hatred, betrayal and slander are dragging him from from one world to another, from the living to the dead . . . When Gonario opens his eyes the fire is out and the embers scarcely whispering.

That same night Genesia Stocchino's sleep was disrupted by an owl. That watchful bird had taken up position on a chestnut tree whose branches brushed her bedroom window. Softly it began to call. Genesia put a pillow over her head and started to pray for sleep, because at the notary's where she was a maid there were feverish preparations for the marriage of his eldest daughter and a mass of work to be done. But the bird did not let up, and to an attentive ear it kept on saying the same thing: martyrs' flesh and prayers, martyrs' flesh and prayers, over and over again . . . And the more Genesia listened, the clearer the words seemed to become. Certainly the news from Libya was not good, and there in the notary's house they were saying that

84

the Italians were like someone having been sold a ewe as young and milk-producing, only to find her to be old and dried up. Martyrs' flesh and prayers. No news of Samuele. A few people who had come back missing a leg or an eye had heard that he was alive, though the Fourth had suffered heavy losses and they said they had been transferred from Benghazi to Tripoli . . . Stormy seas, the owl said unexpectedly . . .

Políto put his nose up close to Samuele's mouth. "He's breathing, he's breathing," he said. Puddu from Oliena moistened Samuele's lips again, as the M.O. had told him to. Tripoli came into view, not far off. The sea seemed turned to stone. In a little while they would get a stretcher ready.

At the army hospital the doctors, like desperate midwives, pulled Samuele out of the womb of death. A miracle, they said, because the chances of surviving a collapsed lung were absolutely minimal. What he needed now was rest, a discharge and home.

"No," pleaded Samuele. "Not a discharge! Convalescent leave at home, but not a discharge. Because I'm going to get well; at home I'll get well."

The duty doctor gave him a doubtful look: "Very well, Stocchino, but with reservations."

"Alright," said Samuele.

So just as soon as he could get to his feet and was able to take a few steps in the army hospital in Tripoli, he was already applying for convalescent home leave.

He arrived in Naples more dead than alive. He spent a week in the infirmary of the Mergellina harbour office and two months in the sanatorium at Pozzuoli. Then one bitterly cold morning, without waiting for permission, he took the first ferry to Sardinia.

*

And now we see him back in the village. It is January 1913. The rest is all in the telling: war stories to Felice, and to Gonario stories of women . . .

IV

Legends and more legends

The First Legend

The first legend tells of how Samuele came home from Libya
more dead than alive. In the first section of the storyteller's
picture he is shown as emaciated, skeletal, tottering about in the
deserted alleys of the village. Next comes a description of his
entry into the house like the ghost of Hamlet's father. Antioca is
washing up, Genesia left some time ago. Gonario has not been
home for four days. Felice is at the olive press for the pressing.
The little savages are at Oristano, thank God.

This is how it seems to have gone: Samuele did not enter
the house, but stopped in the doorway. Antioca recognised him
before he could utter a word, stared wide-eyed at him and put
a hand over her mouth to stifle a shriek. What sort of a son
have they sent back to her?

Without a word she took his hands, led him inside and sat
him down. Samuele let himself be led as if he had no will of his
own, but it was only that he lacked the strength. His eyes looked
huge in the face of a Samuele who was a pale ghost of the lad
who had left two years before. He had the wispy beginnings of a
beard, and his hands were trembling and breathing was an effort.

At last Antioca spoke:

"Child . . ." she murmured.

Samuele sketched a sort of smile, then nodded as if to say
things were not as they seemed, that he was alright really, just
tired.

The second part of the storyteller's picture shows him in bed, like an *ex voto*. It's all there, including the cloud bearing the Madonna and Antioca praying for the health of her son back from the war. At the foot of the bed sits Felice, listening to his son's war stories.

In the pictures that follow, in fact, Samuele is a hero, terror of the infidels, ferocious tiger, bemedalled soldier. Then the story changes because the miracle happens and Samuele recovers. No-one believes it, everyone has given him up for dead and yet . . . a slight gesture from the cloud depicted above the patient's bed and he is on his feet again.

In the middle panel, in vivid colours, we see Samuele lifting his arms skywards and crying out. The day is crystal clear, ablaze with the flowering of an improbable but utterly paradisical springtime. No-one would have thought such a display could exist in nature, and in fact it does not. Even the village of Arzana as it appears in that picture is a Christmas crib of toylike little houses, with all the sweetness of marzipan.

Thus flow the edifying stories of innocent souls while Fate is drawing him ever closer to going on the run.

This happiness lasts for only a moment and bears the face of Mariangela. She found him when he landed up there in the abyss and now she finds him again. He does not yet know it, but even as a little boy he was her chosen one. When they meet again he is as thin as a juniper twig, while she is as round and tiny as a juniper berry. One and the same plant . . .

Then we enter the usual business of happiness disrupted. Yes, because Mariangela is much sought after. Almost at the end of our picture, in a scene at the bottom, we see her scornfully rejecting the attentions of a wealthy landowner. Her expression says: I will not yield. Like certain martyred saints who bear their own organs before them on a tray, yet maintain a distance, almost an indifference, towards the martyrdom which has mutilated them. Mariangela has all that rage, but also that indifference.

In the next picture Samuele is sinking a knife deep into the landowner's chest.

The storyteller comments that the rogue has got his come-uppance: a dahlia of ruby-red blood to adorn his chest. Samuele is simply a hand that strikes, a blade that pierces and smashes through the breastbone. The poor wretch flings wide his arms as if to welcome what was coming to him . . .

The first legend ends here with Samuele saving the honour of Mariangela.

The Second Legend

The second legend is about the indissoluble bond between Samuele and Mariangela. We can see that from her point of view, not so much Christian as pagan, the fact of having heard him calling from down there in the abyss, when they were both scarcely seven years old, meant that they were destined for one another. Or else, to put it better, that he was the one destined for her. The fact is that ever since that day they were saved, right until he set off for Libya nine years later, she had always resolutely declared him to be "hers". Without a word to anyone, of course. But she always kept her eye on him. Then he had enlisted, at only sixteen, by lying about his age.

And at this point the legend becomes a story of faith. When everyone was saying that Stocchino wouldn't come back, that he was one of the many "killed in Libya", she said no. She said it is the unloved who die in war. Everyone who heard that laughed and gave dozens of examples to the contrary: the butcher, the blacksmith's apprentice, the bricklayer . . . All of them loved and dead to a man. She replied that that wasn't enough, that people do die in war if they're loved in "that" way. She said that so as not to die you had to do what she had done and take upon yourself what is usually shared between two. In all the seven months when there was no news of Samuele, Mariangela never left Antioca's side, helping with the washing up and taking the dirty clothes to the wash-trough. As if taking for granted that they were bound together by a love they shared. No-one said it, but she, Mariangela, knew it.

So in January 1913 the spectre of Samuele returned to the village. Mariangela had been right. One might have expected her to claim what had always been her own, but that did not happen. During all the long time when our soldier was confined to bed there was no sign of Mariangela. In her great joy as a mother granted a miracle, Antioca almost did not notice but, without knowing why, she felt something missing at her side.

Samuele's first task on coming back to life was to tell of the inferno he had visited, the goatish features of the crafty Levantine, the manly heroism of the Italic warrior and also, though only in an undertone, between man and man, of his bedroom exploits . . . Then, once he was really on his feet, came the time of small chores. He was now a bemedalled soldier, though not yet nineteen years old. When he left he was Samuele de sos de Crabile, and now he was Corporal Stocchino, with relations who are talked about by the neighbours because they have a hero in the family.

Mariangela kept her distance. Intuition told her that the longer you are able to wait, the greater the reward in the end.

She dreamed continually that when Samuele saw her he returned to the abyss to ask what had become of her and why on earth – since she knew that they were made for one another – she had not come to welcome him when, Lazarus-like, he had returned from the kingdom of death to tell everyone what he had seen there.

But Samuele was not yet aware of that destiny of his. Now that he was feeling himself again, and now that Doctor Milone had baptised him as the child of a miracle, just as soon as he had begun to put one foot in front of the other without fighting for breath, all he thought of was that he had come back to life again.

True enough, his legs were still as shaky as a newborn colt's, but spring was bursting out. They say that he yelled to the sun as a sign of victory.

In her long wait Mariangela had learned to interpret marvels. She had also learned the power of the eyes.

They say that one Friday, on his way to Larentu Sotgiu's farm, Samuele had felt thirsty.

The previous night Mariangela had had a dream about a laughing angel who was urging her to go and fetch water . . . In her dream she did not even deign to answer, because the angel didn't look like a trustworthy person. But the angel, a dirty, toothless shepherd boy, went on telling her that what she had been waiting for had arrived and she had to rush to the pump in the square as quickly as she could. Mariangela had no wish at all to talk about what in her heart she had desired for years, and was outraged at the lad's impertinence, but almost at once where he had been there was only light and fragrance, and a voice repeating: "coming and going, coming and going . . ."

When she woke she was sweating all over, and without a word to anyone she headed straight for Annfca Tola, the only person who could interpret her dream.

The legend has it that this was the very morning when Samuele yelled at the sun and that Mariangela, on her way to Annfca Tola, passed close by him, shading her eyes from the blinding sunlight, and that even though she did not see him she recognised his voice: voice and light, just as in her dream. So she turned back the way she had come, because all there was to be understood she had understood already.

The first thing she understood was that the moment had come. Then she understood that the destiny of her love for

Samuele was a circle, a coming and going . . . She realised she had to prepare herself for the agony of a lover who constantly has to start all over again. She clasped her arms tightly to her breast to stiffen her resolve, for the future was not going to be roses all the way.

Samuele was on his way to Larentu Sotgiu's place, but he felt thirsty, so instead of taking the direct route he made a detour to the piazza, where the pump was. There he saw the back of a woman who was filling a jug . . .

Mariangela had got herself dressed up, had put on her rings as if off to the Feast of the Patron Saint, with a blouse of startling whiteness and her best shawl. When the jug was half full she heard him coming, heard the clatter of the hobnailed army boots. By now Samuele was walking close behind her, but she did not turn. She simply felt him, there at her back, as if he had caressed her. Yet he had done nothing but wait until her jug was full.

"They had given you up for dead, Samuele Stocchino," Mariangela said, still not turning.

"But here I am alive and kicking," he replied, spreading his arms.

"Are you thirsty?" she asked.

He nodded, and she saw him do it even though she couldn't, because she still had her back turned. But now she straightened up and faced him. He was a small fellow, a mere span taller than she was, yet he did not look like a shorty because everything depends on the proportions . . . They were face to face. He looked at her, then raised his eyebrows . . . "If you want to drink, go on and drink," she said, moving aside.

"No, no, fill it up," he said, motioning to the half-full jug.

"Go on and drink," she insisted, as if to say that also for the future their relationship as lovers would mean that his needs always came first.

The legend has it that he, like Jacob when he saw Rachel at the well, at once felt the urge to kiss her. And it tells us that this happened because an absolute conviction had sprung to life within him: that that woman had chosen him from the beginning, and there was nothing he could do to make her change her mind. If you had seen Mariangela's eyes through the eyes of Samuele, you too would have understood.

The corporal bent forward a little, as if to react to a stab in the stomach, *mortu su groddo*. She took a step back to make the point that, adored though he may be, he had to keep his distance. It was an exact geography, with exact boundaries, over which he could not and must never have the least mastery. So he approached and she moved away, then he bent to drink and she lightly brushed his shoulder.

They say that after that meeting they never left each other again.

The Third Legend

The third legend tells of how for a certain time Samuele, there in Arzana, had in his innermost being, in his very entrails, restrained the beast within him. Tiger or wolf as may be. But most of all it tells of the wonder of that moment at the village pump, when our corporal realised he had been pierced through as by a bayonet. This was in August 1914, just a month after Gavrilo Princip had lit the fuse for the outbreak of the Great War.

But for Samuele Stocchino the summer of 1914 was what hagiographers call "the season of perfect peace". It was love's idyll, with everything that ensues. First of all a filter that smoothes out all imperfections, that overwhelms reality. And the reality of the matter was that things were going very badly. Felice was practically paralysed with arthritis. Gonario was moving from one boss to another in search of better employment, which as a hireling shepherd did not even allow him any cigarette money. Even Genesia had troubles with her job at the notary's: too much work and a pittance in return. For the war hero back from Libya there was nothing for it but to do the best he could, wear his uniform and army-issue boots, and put up a good show.

This is the part of the story where something really was about to happen. No-one said a word, because it could not be true that it would all end in an insipid "they lived happily ever after". But this was what Samuele thought he thought. His heart was brim-full of all kinds of prospects. Everything, but everything, seemed to him real and true. After all, for a year now he had made only fleeting visits to the real world and now basked in the warm glow of Mariangela's eyes. A gallant in uniform, therefore all the more gallant, but also a gallant in love, therefore more defenceless.

The story goes on to tell us that Giacomo Manai needed someone to look after his horse. Samuele in his uniform seemed to him no more than a just recognition of his status as the richest man in town. No-one in Arzana called him Manai, they all said "the richest man in town", which he was. So when Samuele presented himself and said he was not afraid of work, the "richest man in town" asked him to take a seat, treated him as civilised people do, and then started off by saying that he really didn't need any more workers, that times were hard, what with the war, and so on and so forth. Samuele pointed out that he knew all about the war, and from very close quarters. So Manai nodded and said that he had in mind a way of employing him without humiliating him, because in fact he needed no more workers, but maybe for Samuele, seeing that he had fought against those savages over there, in short and in a word, he just had to find him something . . .

What he found was looking after a horse, being a groom in fact, or rather the batman of an officer who did not exist but who had a horse. And that horse was more important than any human being. On that score "the richest man in town" would brook no argument. Never mind anything else, his Arab-Sardinian steed had to be in perfect form, well curry-combed, glossy and well fed. Samuele had to act as nursemaid to this horse, but he must never ride him. He must exercise him, stir up the blood in that stallion's very fibres and nourish him as an honoured guest. Manai did not care if the groom had anything to eat or not, all he demanded was that the horse be well fed. And he had his laughs from it too. He insisted on being saluted by that toy soldier he had employed for his beloved animal. But the toy soldier, as we have said, was a toy soldier in love.

The third legend goes on to tell of how Samuele turned the tables. Only a few months before, Manai, just for making fun of him, would have been "the richest *corpse* in town", but now no longer. Autumn was coming on, but when a man is relishing the first real joy of his life he does not listen to what is going on around him. Or else he does, and his ear is only too keen . . .

At this point the storyteller of the third legend pauses and gazes intently at his audience. He wishes to convey that that momentary lapse must perforce be followed by some irrepressible fury. That happiness was only a passing moment in the short life of the tiger of Ogliastra.

And he sums the matter up as follows: he has learned the smell and the taste of blood, he has had visions, he has nourished a beast within him and has then encountered love. An unstable compound, a very tricky mixture.

He does not dwell on that, but goes on to tell of how Samuele led the horse around in his uniform and no-one said a word, and after grooming and feeding the horse he was free to go and meet Mariangela on the outskirts of the village, where the air smelled of elder and burned leaves. And so it was every day at the same hour. Samuele would lead the horse out of the village "to give him a bit of an airing", as he put it. And every time he passed them by, the old men sitting in the piazza would touch their cap brims or bare their heads to make fun of him. Including Manai. Manai most of all, in fact, because he thought he had never made a better buy than to see that bigmouth Stocchino being a nanny to his horse. Moreover, the horse had never been in better condition: rippling muscles and a glossy coat. Led by his groom, the horse had a positively imperial gait. But the joke of it was that Giacomo Manai had failed to notice one small item: he did not cotton on to why the oats in the stable were never finished. It was a complete mystery, seeing how the horse was so well fed . . .

The mystery was solved a week later, when the time came for the potato harvest. In a word, when everyone else was bringing in cartloads of potatoes, Manai had an empty field, simply because while he was having a laugh at Samuele in the piazza, Samuele was having a laugh at him in the potato field, where he took the horse to browse. Well-fed horse, no potatoes, oats uneaten, employer cheated, job lost. At which the whole village had a laugh.

The Fourth Legend

The fourth legend is closely connected to the third. Or rather, it is the direct result of it. Inasmuch as it tells of a joke gone awry. Because we all know that there are people who like to poke fun at others but don't like it the other way round. Like Giacomo Manai, in fact, who had been made a fool of in front of the whole village. This, they say, was the origin of a terrible enmity.

Four days after the horse episode Gonario Stocchino was sacked. His employer told him that he was selling up and didn't need him any more, and in any case he had heard that he was looking around for other work, and therefore . . . Therefore? Gonario almost exploded with rage but he fought to keep calm because in that flock he had seven sheep of his own and if the worst came to the worst he didn't have so much as a scrap of land on which to graze them. So he asked him at least to keep his sheep until he could find a new employer, because being a shepherd was the only job he knew. But things did not turn out well; in fact, far from it. Two weeks later his former employer sent to tell him that he had to take away his sheep because the new owner was not willing to take on the livestock of an ex-employee. And the new owner, needless to say, was Giacomo Manai. So Gonario went to collect his sheep, which he had asked a shepherd at Villagrande to look after in return for occasional work. Better than nothing. When he got to the sheep-fold where he had worked for years, there was Manai in person. Now, Gonario recognised his own sheep perfectly well, but Manai claimed that he was picking out the best of the flock, and as he was lord and master it was up to him to decide which were Gonario's sheep. And in fact he went on to pick out seven of the oldest, two of which were already sterile. Gonario said no, those were not his sheep, that he knew his own sheep one by one.

"Around here you don't even own the air you breathe," pronounced Manai. "Either you agree to take these or else, since I bear you no malice, I'll give you a small price for them."

Gonario saw red, but again by some miracle he managed to keep his temper.

"It's not me you're getting at," he said almost in a whisper. "It's someone else."

Manai gave him a hard look. "This is only the beginning," he said.

Gonario nodded. The owner was surrounded by armed men . . .

On that same afternoon, not far away, Samuele was waiting for Mariangela, because for the first time she wasn't already there at the appointed place. And these are the things that turn one's world upside down. Happiness, which feeds on infinity, on being everlasting, suffers such changes as bitter blows. Nor was Mariangela any better off: she had been forced to stay at home because she was the object of a proposal of marriage. The joke that had gone sour was producing an inexorable series of atrocious results. The women who brought the proposal of marriage to Mariangela's family were the aunt (a nun) and the spinster sister of Battista, second son of Giacomo Manai. His elder brother, Luigi, was standing outside the door.

Samuele waited for two whole hours. To describe him accurately you would have to look closely at his eyes: two pinpoints. Seeing that the tryst was a flop, he left the love nest and walked quickly home. He looked as if he had some impelling urgency, some clear objective, but in fact he had none. It was this that made him regret and curse the day he had stopped being a soldier to become a man.

Never for a moment did it occur to him that Mariangela might not have been able to come to their tryst: he saw only the fact that she was not there. Thus it was that, quite unexpectedly, he found that all his haste really did have an objective. He realised it when he stopped outside Mariangela's house.

She, from inside the house, without knowing how or why, felt him arrive. She understood him so well, and knew what was going on inside him. As for her family, they were all as pleased as could be, because a family bond with the Manai of Arzana really meant something. Nobody asked Mariangela what she felt about it.

For four whole days Samuele did not open his mouth, did not leave the house, did not look at anything further off than his own hands. Antioca, who was wise and could put two and two together, realised that this silence of his was due to what they were saying in the village, that Mariangela's hand in marriage had been requested by Battista Manai. The one everybody called "the halfwit". So she planted herself in front of her son and told him that things happened as they were destined to happen, and that if he and Mariangela had made a secret vow it didn't count, because the only vows that counted were the ones made in the sight of God and in the proper way. At this point, for the first time, Samuele raised his head.

"Yes, it does count," he almost croaked, because he had not spoken for so long and his throat was dry. And at that, according to the fourth legend, the "time of peace", the "happy time", was ended once and for all.

Round and round the wheel of fortune. It isn't finished yet. Felice, slowed down by age and arthritis, comes home out of breath and places on the kitchen table a package and a small sack. In the package is a quarter of a seasoned cheese, three flat fresh cheeses and a handful of carobs. In the sack is his "share" of olives. Antioca has nothing to say, nothing to add: she can do her own sums. The work with the olives is not yet finished, Felice has brought home his tiny share, so he has been dismissed. The olive grove and its yield are the property of Giovanni Bardi, brother-in-law of Giacomo Manai. Need we say more?

It was then that Samuele for the first time sat down at the table to write. His handwriting was as sharp as the teeth of a saw:

> *By this time you all know that certain persons have persecuted me and others of my family . . . And I have started and will continue to be a butcher to these scoundrels. From now on all those who do us harm will be repaid in their own coin by me.*
> *Samuele Stocchino*

Nailed to the church door at Arzana, this note, written on brown wrapping paper, had the same disconcerting effect on the townsfolk as the famous declaration of Martin Luther.

Father Marci sent for Manai. What was said is not reported

in the legend, but the fact is that two days later Giovanni Bardi sent a message to Gonario to tell him that he could stand in for his father for the olive-picking, if he so wished. Gonario accepted.

Then Father Marci sent for Samuele and what he said was that threats are a terrible thing, not only for the receiver but even more so for the threatener.

Samuele shrugged: "Whoever got my threats knows I mean it and has to watch their step," he said between his teeth.

Father Marci drew back a hand as if to slap Samuele's face.

"You want to act grown up but you're still just a boy," he said. "I am simply warning you, but those are people who could gobble you up, you and your whole family, so mind what you say, because this time I'll let it go but if you do it again I'll stuff your notice down your throat . . . Understand?" And they say that Samuele kept his eyes on the ground as if he really had become a child again. "Listen here. Manai has taken it calmly because he respects me. Otherwise you'd have got a thrashing for what you've done."

Still not a word from Samuele.

The Fifth Legend

The fifth legend is written in blood. When everything seemed resolved, when what had to be said had been said, when the breaking point had been clearly defined, when the territories had been marked out. At Arzana there was a terrible silence surrounding the enmity between Manai and Stocchino. When something is talked about, it means there is still something to say, but when people stop talking about it, that means things have taken a turn for the worse.

And in fact the fifth legend is all a hissing of whispers. Nothing is clear, but everything has a reason behind it. And this time the reason bears the name of Mariangela. With her hand promised to that halfwit Battista Manai she was forced to hide herself away. This drove Samuele out of his mind, but she begged him to keep calm, because they would marry her to *that one there* over her dead body.

Samuele said nothing.

All the same, Battista Manai was found dead a few days later. So the fifth legend returns to the first legend, in which it was rumoured that Samuele had ripped open the chest of the man who had made an attempt on his woman and eaten his heart.

But no-one had time to bring any official charges. Italy's entry into the Great War had called up the Sardinian pack of hounds and among them was Corporal Stocchino.

This time it was on the Carso.

V

*In which we tell of the night before
setting off to war*

Mariangela laid her white hand on the coverlet. In silence, so as not to wake him. Her tapering fingers so white as to be almost shining. The light touch of her palm travelled up Samuele's back as far as his shoulders. Under the rough fabric of his shirt his flesh was burning hot. With the murmur of a sleepy child, Samuele shook his head on feeling that cold touch on his skin. Now she was stroking the freshly shaved nape of his neck, then the neck itself, lowering her head to breathe upon it. She had her bodice unlaced, did Mariangela. Samuele rolled onto his back, his eyes still closed. He freed his hands from the bedclothes and held both her breasts. As he groped, his breath was heaving. He parted his lips in longing for those breasts, scenting their fragrance in the air. Only then did the woman's face appear. Her skin was slashed with wounds, her eye sockets no more than two oozing pits. Her lips had been knifed off, showing a monstrous grin. The sliced flesh of her skull fell onto her shoulders like an enormous coral-coloured wig. He started up in the bed and closed his eyes tight. Mariangela was mouthing soundless words from the great slit in her throat. His heart thumping, his throat parched, Samuele reached out a hand to his side. He heard the regular breathing of a woman. He thrust his hand into her raven-black hair, and oh, the relief of it.

At his touch she murmured, "A bad dream, my angel," without turning round. And that is what it must have been. He looked around him and the room was empty. "Come back and lie beside me, I'm cold," she begged.

Samuele laughed at himself and his terror. "It was all so real," he told her. "It all seemed so real."

He clung tight to Mariangela's body. And he felt the icy cold that had flooded through her. He shivered at that touch, but could not break free of it. He moved away towards the empty side of the bed, feeling that the woman's limbs had turned into the hard spurs of a petrified plant. He opened his mouth to cry out, but no sound came. But Mariangela had now turned round, without releasing him from her embrace, and had an endless number of arms and hands that ran all over his body. She had lanced through the shirt over his chest and was slashing at him with a tongue as sharp as a stiletto.

He leaped out of bed with a yell, soaked all over with sweat and terror.

He saw no movement from the tangled bedclothes, and it was only then, in the full moonlight, that he could be sure he was alone.

Antioca found him face down on the floor in a fit of shivers. His moans had woken her.

"In God's name, what happened?" she cried, as she came in by the flickering light of a candle. As soon as he saw her, Samuele pulled himself together. He sat up with his arms clasped round his knees. His mother came up to him and put her candle down on a chair. "It was just a bad dream," she said. "It's all over now." And she stroked his head as she hadn't done since he was a child. "*Un'amimutadura, coro meu*," she whispered.

Samuele abandoned himself in her arms. He allowed himself to be led back to bed and tucked in by those expert hands. And he began to relax. For there had been a time (and his memories of it suddenly flashed upon him now) when he could recognise his mother's footsteps outside his room. And he could imagine her listening there in the doorway to make sure that all was well. There had been a time when she had the odour of milk and her skin had the smoothness of balsamic oils. And later, when they told her he must have died out there in the woods, eaten by the animals that haunt the night-time, he could hear the chattering of her teeth. But he very well remembered the day he was brought back to the world of the living, rescued from the depths of the rock, with his flesh sticking to his bones and only enough strength left to swallow a little honey and water. A resurrection which everyone credited to the good will of the Virgin Mary towards the son of Antioca Leporeddu, who had prayed for him. There were no doubts that it had been an answer to a prayer, a clear sign of God's design to obliterate the word "*finis*".

Antioca stayed there a minute or two, watching her son's face beginning to relax again. Then she slowly backed away to pick up her candle.

"It all seemed so real," said Samuele suddenly, breaking the silence.

Antioca stepped back to his bedside. "Bad dreams always seem to be real," she said faintly. Then she saw her son's uniform on the chair, all clean and freshly ironed. "Get a few hours' sleep," she said. "Tomorrow will be a long day."

Yes, it was a long journey from Terranuova to Naples for the clearing process. And to join his unknown companions. Irredentists!

PART THREE

Terrified, Caked with Mud, Crazed with
Fear . . . Oh, Terrible!!!

Orders are orders: the High Command had
no need to convince us of it.

Max Frisch, *Service Record*

Voice from the Wings

There was a time, not all that long ago, when that same moon, launched into the night as into the centre of a stage, still had a virginal look. There was a time when she approached so close to the earth as to seem one all-embracing light which made you dizzy to look at and gave a strange feeling of distress and languor, of fear and pleasure. A pleasure very like pain.

A god before God had danced, immersed in that lustre, when it was thought that the stamp of his feet would awaken lifeless matter, in the night of nights, when everything was still to be made. When it was thought that it needed only a dance to awaken the sleepy body of the earth. When it was thought it needed only a dance to endow it with the marvel of flowers to adorn it and of moving bodies to inhabit it. When they propitiated the lightning and the earthquakes and the stormy winds. When every act had to be in perfect keeping with the cosmos. And every word had to have a sound so tuned as not to offend the touchy beast. And every step had to be an image of the god who danced it. So that the bleating of the ram and the bellowing of the bull, the crackling of flames and the rippling of water could together produce a harmony which was music indeed, but at the same time a map of the stars: an account of the firmament, an imitation of the skies on the earth.

For this reason, on such a night as this, the earliest of us arranged ourselves in a circle to act out the whirling passage of time and of the planets. The earliest of us came together to agree on a rhythm and apportion the parts: you are the ram, you are the bull, you are the fire, you are the water.

It was enough to make us feel divine, so close to the primal meaning of things as to think one was yet unborn. Enough to make us feel immortal.

On such a night as that of the killing, all prayers had been answered. Matter had awoken and, like a wet dog shaking itself, had sprinkled the sky with an infinite number of burning brands.

The earliest of us had swum up to the surface, had groped their way onto dry land, crossed the swamps and found a home. And thus they had risen to their feet, still as shaky as newborn foals. They had raised their arms in imitation of the branches of trees and howled to try out their lungs.

Consciousness arrived like a smack in the face.

For it is hard to bestow a meaning on so many thousands of years of massive suffering. Often we cannot find words for it, but there remains within us a memory which is empty.

That is how it came about.

Or anyway, that is what they tell us. And they go on to say that pride incited the first of us to multiply, so in love were they with their own image, and incited them to die, because this meant returning to the exact point of departure, to the glory of petrified clay, to the inviolable effigy of the Mother. To the centre of centres.

Dazzled by the soundless light they left this earth as if they were dancing. But only to begin over again, because the moon was persistent and so was the sun, and persistent also was the hope of perpetuating that cry and that consciousness.

They say that it happened by night, a night like that of the killing, when pride, in the long running on of time, had become a little, pale, flickering flame. Because the planet of self-love had become a satellite, a whirling speck on the edge of the universe. Because the thread of memory had become so tangled that they could no longer find their way through the labyrinth of themselves.

The last of us, naked, were wandering over the sleeping earth, shielding their faces from the glare because, on the night of the killing, there was a full moon and a strange, tormenting euphoria . . . Very like a pain.

I

Service record

*We eat the dirt here, and the rats eat us. Unless we start eating them.
Never seen such huge rats: they attack dogs and even us Christians.
We can see their point: after all, in the manoeuvring for position
the rats occupied the territory long before the Krauts. And I can
assure you that when cooked to a turn they aren't half bad, either
the rats or, still less, the Krauts. Up on the Podgora the rats are a
delicacy: because of road works supplies have been held up for
sixteen days. But there are a few lucky ones who have a protective
net over their bunks. Oh yes, the rats are more scary than the
shells. They make not a sound, and they nibble at your nose and
ears while you are asleep. The M.O. says that they possess a serum
that prevents you from feeling the bite of their teeth into your flesh.
You get to understand a lot of things while you're waiting there
defenceless in the trenches. It's like a foretaste of death and burial.
The taste of earth. And you also realise, for example, how important
it is to be able to write. Ah yes, thay say that what you need in war
are courage and proper weapons, but those things don't fit the bill.
In this war, writing is as vital as good equipment. We see every day
what getting letters from home does to the morale of the fellows
who get them; but to get letters you also have to know how to write
them. That, yes. Anyone who never got letters from home seemed
dead even before being heaved out of the trenches. Dead in memory,
with no means of expressing themselves, a death of fear, of cold
and of nausea. For the first days it seemed really and truly impossible to survive, but then, with enough grappa inside you, you grasp*

the most important thing: you don't need willpower. Not even the will to survive.

Samuele had learned this only too well as a veteran of the Libyan campaign and also as a civilian back at home: survival is not willpower, but simply a matter of defiance. And he had defied forces that would have destroyed almost anyone. On the ship en route for Tripoli, for example, he was more dead than alive and before that in the abyss . . . This relentless defiance was the weapon that had made him immortal, an invisible armour encasing him.

Here, too, it was all a matter of holding one's positions, the Austrians on the mountain top, the Italians on the lower slopes. But all without exception in armed occupation of Ratland. Captain Trestini, who came from Livorno, said that there were at least seven rats to every soldier, and that it would have been far more sensible to decide the matter with a battle between the Italian and the Austrian rats. But anyway, war was war, nothing to be done about it, they couldn't go off on holiday.

To Samuele, the discomforts of military life seemed almost normal. Even in Africa it had been the same, but for the freezing cold instead of the stifling heat. And also the fact that here on both sides of the front they crossed themselves before going in to attack.

Here in our unit we are mostly Sardinians, worse than in Libya, worse than in Babel, because there are those from Ozieri who are "Tuscanised", as Lieutenant-Colonel Barzini says, and Frenchified ones from Orune. The former with the aspirated "c", the latter with the French "r". In our buried world you hear every sort of lingo. We who are from Nuoro, Oliena, Mamoida, Orgosolo, keep pretty much to ourselves. Almost no-one from Arzana, but three from Jerzu and ten from Ulassai. Even one from Tortoli, but then it emerged he was only born there and had lived all his life in Sassari, where all the nobs come from.

Here in the trenches we learn there are places in Sardinia we'd never heard of. You think you're pretty knowledgeable, but as a rule you don't know much. One lad told us he came from Luna Matrona and we all laughed, because there couldn't be a place with that name in Sardinia. But he insisted that it wasn't all that far from Barumini and everyone nodded: yes, Barumini with all those nuraghe, but Luna . . . Luna what? And more laughs.

Just as well we can laugh from time to time, even here where there's bloody little to laugh about. As soon as we got to Monfalcone they told us it was a matter of weeks, that in a month at the outside we'd be in Trieste, and it's been two years now . . .

Samuele learned of Felice's death in a letter from Father Marci. The first of two letters he received in the whole duration of the war. Felice and Cecco Beppe died at the same time. Samuele thought silence a sufficient homage to such a silent father.

He kept the news to himself, for Father Marci had not explained or told him anything. He had merely sent an announcement, in keeping with the fact that he had become a priest. To announce a death was for him like saying good morning, because he had signed a contract which stipulated that death was not a grievous matter, but a certainty. So what do you answer to an announcement of that sort? Nothing.

Samuele knocked back a gulp of grappa. They had strict orders not to stint on that, because it warms you up.

The trenches of the two fronts were very close. A hundred metres uphill you could see the heads of the Austrians, and if any one of them popped up it became target practice. The same on both sides. Poddighe from Orani, for example, whiled away the time doing just that. He aimed and fired, and every time an Austrian helmet blew off he cut another notch in his rifle butt. Until he got something in return which made him think again. "Oh, give over," scolded Puddu from Oliena. He and Samuele had known each other since Libyan days. And here they met again on the Carso.

As a matter of fact, when Puddu saw Samuele he almost had a heart attack, he thought he had seen a ghost. "Stocchino!" he croaked. "What! You still alive?"

Samuele gave his balls a squeeze, then made the fig gesture at him.

"Right before your eyes!" he replied, and they threw their arms around each other.

"I'd heard nothing of you since they carted you off to hospital in Tripoli and if you're not a dead man that must mean you're really a bad 'un, to have such a charmed life."

Samuele gave him a grin, in one hand clenching the letter from Father Marci.

"Until it's your time to go . . ." he said, with a sort of an air of wisdom that well became his face. Which was leaner, but not hollow-cheeked. Samuele was of the type who want to keep up a good front in the face of adversity. His bit of a beard roughened his jaw, but to be honest it could not really be called a beard: more a kind of smudge. Rather like the clumsy shading you expect from a pavement artist.

I have always wondered how it is these things happen. This cold, for example, how is it that I ended up in that tomb without being dead yet? They say it was a howitzer shell. I only know that I felt as if a hand had lifted me into the air. One moment I was chatting with Puddu and the next there I was underground, just like my father. I realised I was alive because I could lift my arm and could hear someone stirring.

*

113

All that earth became a tomb. Once out of the chasm that had engulfed him, Samuele was able to tell a story he knew only too well: the story of the mortal rejected by death. It had not turned out that way for others. Curreli of Gavoi, Petrella of Guspini, Mereu of Aggius . . . these had not answered at roll call. "Puddu, where are you?" he started shouting as he shook the soil from on top of him. The skimming searchlights, which were a help but also offered a target, made the ground look like boiling mud.

Samuele got to his knees. All that could be seen of his face were the whites of his eyes and, had he smiled, the gleam of his teeth. But he was not smiling. He was crawling on all fours towards what was left of the Italian trench.

"*Puddu, bi sese?*" he called again.

Puddu answered, then coughed. They had been face to face wishing each other luck and had been hurled at least thirty yards apart.

"*Eja, tottu bene . . .*" Puddu replied.

This was the way with these Sardinians, that after every explosion, after every action, when silence fell someone would get just to their knees, so as not to be a target for snipers, and start to call the roll. Sometimes it happened, in the hazards of war which mix up all the cards and muddle the game, that the call of a shepherd from Gallura might be answered by a shepherd from Carinthia. Because those calls have no respect for nationality and answer to no high command. However, talking in Sardinian was for many soldiers the only chance of communicating. Communicating without being understood by all the others, but not for group solidarity, or not for that only. It was, first and foremost, for lack of an alternative. To the mainlander officers this incomprehensible speech sounded like silence, but it was no such thing; it was a constant hum, speech in an undertone that in the ganglions of the front-line trenches provided a bass drone for the shrill crackle of machine guns . . .

So it was that whenever they deigned to visit the front line the top-brass generals always asked the same question:

"How is it that these Sardinians never utter a word?"

"They talk alright, sir, it's just that they talk among themselves."

The general would give the Sardinian dogs a good looking-over; they were just the right size, stumpy and solid, perfect for going over the top against enemy fire. They only needed to advance head down as if walking into a stiff wind and there was a good chance the line of fire would be too high to hit them. In addition to that they never gave up, never spoke, or rather spoke only among themselves, which was just the same as saying nothing, wasn't it?

From early May until the end of June of 1916 the grind went on. There was no stopping it. We were all aiming towards Gorizia, but the Austrians attacked from the Trentino in our rear. Gorizia fell in August, but in our rearguard it was a relentless massacre. If you fell back you were lost, but you were lost even if you advanced. At the nation's chopping-block General Cadorna thumped his fists. Soldiers were killing soldiers, and not only their enemies.

Samuele, being one for obeying the rules, understood all this. He was someone who had had to work to gain the respect of his townsfolk. Then the letter arrived:

"Felice dead, in peace with Almighty God, may he be with the just, Amen."

From the enemy trenches could be heard laments for the death of Franz Josef, and Samuele in his inmost mind thought those cries a worthy tribute to Felice's tormented life.

So then there was Puddu from Oliena, then the explosion . . .

And you started all over again.

II

In which we tell of an unexpected encounter

Gorizia was taken only in a manner of speaking, deserted and infested with snipers. You had to sidle along the walls and as for going on horseback, forget it. Therefore the orders were for mopping up. In other words, patrolling the city inch by inch and firing on sight at anything that moved. After all that time huddled in the trenches, the wide open spaces of the city were a little scary: too much light, everything too human. We were an army of moles burrowing through the skeleton of a city. Better off half-buried, filching food from the rats.

On the opposite front, up on the "plateau", the infantry had somehow to stem the advance of the Krauts in the Trentino to prevent them flooding down into the Veneto. Samuele was put in charge of a soldier who had been sentenced to be shot. He was a twenty-year-old from Ulassai, found unconscious in a barn during a reconnaissance, and the sergeant, who came from Frosinone, declared he was a deserter. To Samuele he seemed just a child who had lost his way, but the orders were to keep him under guard until he "came to his senses". Ever since Cadorna had thumped his fists on the table every drunken twenty-year-old had become a deserter. So the sergeant from Frosinone left Samuele with the soldier and went off to H.Q. to put in train a request for execution. He did not want to take full responsibility, so to be on the safe side he started the official procedure. Samuele thought that this army had become like a frightened child in the hands of a parent incapable of dealing with him.

Anyway, the little soldier woke up five minutes after everyone else had left, sat up suddenly and asked what had happened.

Samuele spread his arms: "Don't you know what you've done?"

The lad looked around blankly. He could not think of anything that might have got him into trouble. Certainly he'd lifted his elbow a little, but it was the New Year, wasn't it?

"That's right," agreed Samuele. "First of January, 1917."

"Happy New Year," said the other.

"Happy?" said Samuele. "What's happy about it? Don't you realise they mean to shoot you?"

The lad's face turned chalk white. "Why? What for?" he asked.

He had gone off with a woman, a very nice woman, they'd had a spot to drink, whooped it up . . . He had missed roll call, and orders are orders.

So tears of desperation burst forth as soon as the soldier from Ulassai realised that without a shadow of doubt he was a dead man, and that where they had brought him there was no time, no New Year, let alone a happy one . . .

Samuele could find no response to the other's weeping, an outburst of real, howling, angry, hysterical weeping, perhaps because it was something that required no response. So he knelt down until the tip of his nose was touching the nose of the other.

"Give me a wallop," he whispered, as if he feared someone might overhear.

The other stared in amazement. "Where are you from?" he asked.

"Arzana," replied Samuele.

"Ulassai," said the other. "Rubanu," he added.

"Stocchino," said Samuele.

Time was running out. Rubanu got to his feet, Samuele stayed kneeling.

*

117

When he came round he realised they had taken him to the field hospital. The sergeant from Frosinone was raging at Samuele for having let himself be tricked by a raw recruit. Samuele was glad of this, because at least he did not suspect it had been deliberate. In any case, disciplinary action against him was a matter for Captain Lussu.

Captain Lussu was long and stringy, the tallest man you ever saw. His very look was terrifying. Samuele, standing before him with bandaged head, saluted and gave his name and number. The captain told him to take a seat and eyed him for a long time.

"Samuele Stocchino, Arzanesu," he said, "Ogliastrono, eh? Great place, Ogliastra . . . Plenty of good shooting. Crafty people, too," the captain added, glaring at Samuele with his glowing eyes. Samuele did not return the look, but he felt it as if it had been poured onto him. "So tell me exactly what happened."

Samuele gave a shrug. He sighed. "What can I say, Captain? He took me by surprise."

"By surprise," echoed Captain Lussu with the ghost of a smile. "And how was that?"

He appeared to be enjoying himself.

"Er . . . from behind."

"Yes, yes, from behind, but how?" insisted the captain. "Show me how . . ." And Samuele began to feel uneasy.

"Come closer," said the captain, beckoning him.

Samuele got to his feet. Standing face to face, the captain and the corporal looked rather like a cypress overshadowing a juniper bush.

"He got me here," said Samuele, pointing to the nape of his neck. "I thought he was still unconscious . . ."

"Whereas Rubanu from Ulassai was not unconscious . . ."

"No."

"And what am I expected to do? Must I tell the general that

118

Ulassai and Arzana are practically next-door neighbours? For all he knows they might be miles apart."

Samuele gave another shrug. "Perhaps you don't need to tell him. What does it matter to him? To the general, that is . . . with all due respect."

"Ah . . . what does it matter to him, eh? Now, are you the fellow who's always shouting in the trenches, the one who calls out to the dead?"

"I try to find the living. Too late for the dead . . ."

"Right, now get out of my sight. And next time, watch it. Go on then, hop it!"

Samuele felt the captain's gaze pouring down his back.

"How is it these Sardinians never talk?"

"They talk, they talk, General. It's just that they talk among themselves."

"But you can't understand a word . . ."

"Not a word, General, but they're good lads, really good lads. Anyway, there aren't only Sardinians here, there are the volunteers as well."

"O Lord, they're a fine lot I must say, all intellectuals . . . Either Sardinians or intellectuals. In either case you can't understand what they're saying."

"Of course you are right, General, and you must also bear in mind that there are Sardinian intellectuals . . ."

Three days after that first meeting between Samuele Stocchino and Captain Lussu, the captain sent for him. The cypress tree towered once more in the middle of the provisional office.

"Come in, come in, Stocchino. I want you to do me a favour." Samuele waited for him to go on. "I'm sending you to Priaforà where we have a problem with a lad from your part of the world . . ." It flashed upon Samuele that they must

119

have caught Rubanu from Ulassai, which meant real trouble. "There's a car waiting for you. When you get there, you'll understand . . ."

Those last words were more than a dismissal. They meant "get going and take care not to make a fool of me". Samuele saluted and found the car outside.

It was about twenty kilometres to Monte Priaforà. A journey through a world of steel. Beneath a sky that looked like a sheet spread out to dry. There were alder trees in these parts and great expanses of heather, and woods of beech trees mingled with silver firs . . .

Samuele said that while the car was climbing, at a height of about eight hundred metres, he leaned out of the window to look at a grazing flock of sheep. They were well-fed sheep with curly white coats, quite different from the scrawny, yellowish animals he knew at home, yet his heart missed a beat. And at that moment he felt a kind of elation that was very like a pain. It all seemed as though war had never touched that little corner of the world.

But it did not last. As soon as they had rounded a bend, there came an explosion. A sheep had touched off a mine. The blast caught the car and the driver almost lost control. But that was the least of it, because a moment later the vehicle was hit by flying chunks of carrion. A lamb fell from on high onto the bonnet. Samuele gaped: God Almighty, history was repeating itself. The driver swerved quickly and got the car under cover. Bits and pieces of sheep were hung in the trees or stuck between the rocks. "Well, I'll be damned," the driver kept saying. "Well, I'll be damned." Samuele's heart was thumping so hard he could scarcely draw breath. A sheep's head was staring at him from the ditch. He had seen enough explosions before, and he had seen solid bodies fly to pieces in the air, but he had never before seen a portent come true. It was this that scared him.

However, after checking that there was no serious damage to the car, they started uphill again. The landscape seen through the windows was now tinged with red: a suitable colour, thought Samuele. His breathing had returned to normal, but he still felt a terrible pang in the pit of his stomach.

Towards the summit they began to spot the positions of the heavy artillery dominating the valley. The whole landscape was almost indecently naked.

They arrived at their destination.

Earthworks were under way. Infantrymen in shirtsleeves were carrying buckets of earth from the mouth of a tunnel. They were digging, they told him, but now they couldn't go on. A sergeant approached.

"He's in there," he said, thinking he had explained everything. Samuele put him right with a look. "The new lad, the Sardinian," explained the other. "We were carrying on with the excavation when he suddenly started raving and put his rifle barrel in his mouth."

Samuele remembered Captain Lussu's face and that "don't make a fool of me", unspoken but as clear as daylight. So without listening to another word he began to call out.

"Ahohhh!"

Nothing. No answer.

"Ahohhh, where are you? Who are you?" he called again, taking no notice of all the men staring at him. And meanwhile he had reached the mouth of the tunnel. "Ahohhh!" he repeated, as if summoning a flock of sheep. And it was as if his premonition back there on the road became clear to him: in his personal apocalypse, sheep and lambs came raining from on high. In his personal book of destiny it set in motion something terrible. But he had no time to think it out now, it was just something that settled in his heart, and that was that.

"Ahohhh!" came a voice from the end of the tunnel and then a beam of light.

Samuele followed it as if beckoned. He took a few steps forward, shielding his eyes with his hand. "Lower that lantern," he said, making his way forward until he could hear the soldier's heaving breath. And the soldier, as if programmed to obey, lowered it. Now the only light in the tunnel was an orange glow reflected off the ground.

The soldier is huddled at the end of the tunnel, his back against the wall, a rifle held between his knees, the barrel in his mouth and his thumb on the trigger. And all this seems almost normal; simply the result of a turmoil such as war, which uproots you from one place to go and "liberate" another which you didn't even know of. And that demands no conscious act. Indeed, the soldier pointing his gun into his mouth knows nothing about anything at all. He can think of no valid reason for his being there in the bowels of the mountain.

All that can be accepted. What cannot be accepted, what turns things upside down, comes when you clearly see that life is an infinite series of recurrences. What strikes is not so much the atrocious silence which has fallen on that tunnel as the complete awareness that something extraordinary is about to happen. Samuele already realised that that day announced by his personal apocalypse could not be just a day like any other. And in fact, now that his sight had become accustomed to the darkness, he could see the soldier's face. And what he saw made him almost crumble at the knees.

"What's your name?" he asked, terrified of the reply.

The other looked at him for a moment and firmly grasping the gun barrel he removed it from his mouth.

"Crisponi," he said in an undertone, as if that name had occurred to him only at that very moment.

"Luigi?" asked Samuele, his throat tightening.

Luigi Crisponi gave a nod. Samuele fell to his knees and clapped a hand over his mouth. He knew that without some decisive action tears would get the better of him. Luigi Crisponi peered at him closely: "Stocchino," he murmured, as if it were something so difficult to imagine that it had almost to be whispered. Samuele nodded, his eyes streaming with silent tears. How long had it been? Fifteen years? Yes, fifteen years.

They embraced.

Maybe that embrace between Luigi and Samuele is all that may be said.

"Child . . ." said Luigi, breaking away. "Child," he repeated, "I have seen so many things about you." And he said it as if he knew things that no-one else was allowed to know. As if he were not even human but some special entity sent there into the bowels of the mountain, as a warning. Samuele was speechless with emotion, a lump in his throat far, far too large to swallow. But Luigi now appeared as calm as could be, while even in the midst of his sobbing Samuele realised that he hadn't changed. He was twenty now, of course, but he still had the attributes of childhood.

"Where have you been?" he managed to ask after a while.

Luigi attempted a smile and leaned back against the rock: "I have been in a place that cannot be described," he said. And that was all.

Silence.

"Everything alright?" called the sergeant from the tunnel mouth. Samuele gave Luigi a questioning look and called back, yes.

"I've seen you die, Samuele," said Luigi out of the blue. "You were on Tanino Moro's land and they shot you in the back, from the pigsty."

"It wasn't me you saw," replied Samuele to encourage him. "I have nothing against Tanino Moro . . ."

"Child," repeated Luigi, like someone trying to restore another to reason.

"Let's go now," Samuele urged gently. "Heavens, how you've had everybody worried."

Luigi gave a slight shrug, started to get up, but then slumped back against the rock wall where he had been at first. He seemed about to get to his feet, but he was only putting the gun barrel back in his mouth.

If you had heard it from outside it would have seemed no more than the bursting of a paper bag. The bullet, trapped by his helmet and the rock into doing the rounds of Luigi's grey matter, left only a faint, dark-red smear on the rock wall. Apart from that, as from a water bottle peppered with shot, the blood trickled down his neck and his back, seeping down between the skin and the rock at his back.

When three or four men rushed into the tunnel Samuele did not even hear what they were were going on about. He was eating the dust, beating his head on stone. The sounds that came out of him were not even cries . . .

They all saw what had happened, and dared not approach.

III

In which we see that when one war ends another begins

And so on compassionate grounds he was sent to the Bainsizza. And there, unsuccessfully, Samuele tried to die. It was a year of terrible bloodshed, 1917, but a perfect climate for anyone who has decided beyond a shadow of doubt that it is not worth going on suffering. Not even the thought of Mariangela did much to cheer him up, though at his worst moments it was his only way of feeling slightly better: grappa and Mariangela. Numbing of the brain and heart. Because falling in love, as he now saw with that cynicism which had dug a groove between his eyes, is just another terrible way to lose oneself. Certainly on the battlefield it is easy enough to bluff with Lady Death, maybe by baring one's breast, defenceless, destroyed by existence itself. Out there it is enough to tell the lady that dying would be a pleasure. The Libyan lion now seemed a pallid shadow of the seducer he had been in the desert. He had become a body devoted to death, absent from himself, ready to kill and to die. Without discrimination. The officers liked this, but it scared the N.C.O.s. So it happened that that body devoted to death spoke little, and when he did it was to offer to die somewhere. Thus the "little corporal" became a kind of mythical figure, but mythical for people who did not know, who could not even imagine, how far Stocchino was from being heroic. He and he alone knew that it did not take much courage to throw oneself into the arms of Lady Death. He had a rage within him that persuaded him that he had all of a

125

sudden become insensible to any pain. Until he received the second letter.

The arrival of the mail in the trenches is one of those times when men feel most alone. Some soldiers read their letters aloud for the benefit of those who have not received one. It was a suggestion from H.Q. because it was thought, rightly for once, that having no news from home lowers the morale of the troops. The propaganda department also encouraged civilians to write. So you found illiterate parents writing to illiterate sons. Some of the soldiers were fairly schooled and read the letters of the illiterate ones written for their parents by a public scrivener. But none of this applied to Samuele. He did not get letters and nor did he write them, although he could have done so. He was one of those who prefer not to know. Anyway, Mariangela could not write and nor could Gonario, and what's more if you got messages at the front it spelled trouble, because bad news travels swiftly but good news is a slowcoach. When he had got that letter from Father Marci nearly a year before, he thought at once that something bad had happened, and sure enough it had. So when he heard the recruit on post duty call out his name he thought it must be a mistake. But it wasn't. It was a well-written letter, as he could tell from the envelope: Samuele Stocchino, etc., etc. There was no doubt about it.

In short, he collected his letter, but did not open it at once like the rest of them, who would tear open the envelope before even finding a place to sit. Inside they would find photographs, sometimes of children, sometimes of girls, at other times of old folks, but at the sight of them they never failed to cry. Samuele put his letter in his pocket. Every so often he fingered it, felt that it was slim, that it had to be a matter of a few words.

WATCH OUT STOCCHINO BECAUSE HERE YOUR
SWORN ENEMIES ARE STEALING ALL YOUR
BELONGINGS AND ARE TAKING ADVANTAGE OF
YOUR SAP OF A BROTHER AND OF YOUR WIDOWED
MOTHER . . . AND YOUR ENEMIES ARE GIACOMO
MANAI, GIOVANNI BARDI AND ALSO EMERENZIANO
BOI WHO ARE DOING WHATEVER THEY WANT . . .

This he read and re-read, over and over again. And he found that somewhere hidden within him was a sluggish streak of rancour. He discovered that that impotent rage, that existence we bear with us, was the bitter fruit of a plant rooted in envy. Get rid of this poison. He spat on the ground – spittle mixed with blood from gums afflicted with pyorrhoea on account of the bad food and hygiene. However, he realised he was now truly in danger: now all he wanted was to get home.

Captain Lussu gave him the thumbs-down, so absurd was the request he had made. Health leave? Inflammation of the lungs? At a moment like this? Did he know what had happened at Caporetto? Leave, be damned! Right here and now the orders were to shoot deserters on sight. Things here either have to turn around or it's the end. Hadn't he been keeping his eyes open? Hadn't he seen the seventeen-year-olds called up? What the hell did he mean by asking for leave? Get out of my sight, Stocchino, get out of my sight!

Ah, Lady Death, he thought he could escape along the side roads, but it was not to be: that lady can only be escaped by sticking to the main highway. By giving a great heave, in the words of General Diaz, who had replaced Cadorna after the rout of Caporetto.

*

And now we hasten to the spring of 1918, because everything that can be told from October 1917 on has already been said. Samuele was selected as one of a corps of special assault troops, death-lovers to a man. Who but him? And the great heave came off because this Diaz had a stick in one hand but a carrot in the other. And the front line on the Piave held like a steel chain. The ones who sank the *Santo Stefano* on 19 June are now called the "Arditi". And so are the men of the Tenth Regiment who crushed the Krauts on the Piave.

Genesia cried every time she told the story. Samuele had ignored the danger, she said, and without waiting for his mates had crawled to an Austrian artillery emplacement, cut the throat of the machine gunner, seized control of the weapon and mown down the enemy. And as if that wasn't enough, he had hoisted the machine gun on his shoulder along with their regimental flag and carried them back to the Italian lines.

When they pinned the gold medal for valour to his breast and promoted him to sergeant, Samuele's sole thought was that he had got halfway along the road home. And in fact his special leave did not take long to arrive.

At Arzana he was greeted with festoons and the town band. The hero of the Piave returning to the bosom of his people. The family were in the front row. Antioca had white streaks in her hair and Gonario was brim-full of bad cheap wine. Genesia looked like a lay sister fresh from the sacristy. The notary's wife had dressed her in pale grey and given her the day off. The twins were there as well, the brothers Samuele scarcely knew, brought up by better-off relations in Oristano. And there were also the shades of Grandmother Basilia and of all those carried off by suffering, or Spanish Flu, before they had a chance to grow up. Felice was missing. He lay in the cemetery. But Father Marci was present, with all the buttons on his cassock shifted because he had grown so fat . . . And they were there as well: Giacomo Manai, Giovanni Bardi and even Emerenziano Boi, the cooper who no longer made barrels but wine to put into them. All three appeared in public as men who could do whatever they wanted. As said in the letter. They all shook Samuele by the hand and gave him a kiss on the cheek.

"Let's forget what has passed between us," whispered Manai with his lips at Samuele's cheek.

There was no reply from Samuele.

"Good health and wealth," whispered Giovanni Bardi.

"I hope the same for you," replied Samuele.

"May you live a hundred years," whispered Emerenziano Boi with some embarrassment.

"Same to you," replied Samuele, when he raised his head to look him straight in the eye.

War was declared.

IV

A bad mistake

And in fact it was only two days before the triumphant home-coming and general carousing for the hero of Arzana became a thing of the past.

Gonario did not have a single sheep left to his name. This was because he had pawned them for a piece of grazing land that he was forced to give up on account of a snag in the contract that he had not understood in the slightest. The house had died along with Felice. Antioca did her best, but it was hard to live on wild salad and scraps of beef. Sometimes a few eggs in exchange for wild asparagus, and a handful of sprats when the fishmonger was about to close shop. She lived in only part of the house, because most of it the landlord had claimed back and thereafter kept closed up.

"How did it happen?" Samuele kept asking.

"Ehhh . . ." Antioca replied every time, spreading her arms.

"Very well," Samuele assured her. "Leave it to me."

"Leave it to me" was something Antioca really had no wish to hear. And this for many reasons, the foremost of which was that there was something she had not yet told Samuele. She had not told him that in about November 1917 the village had given him up for dead.

It is not exactly clear how this misunderstanding came about, but at any rate a survivor from the front who had lost both legs had told a mutual friend at Tortoli that Stocchino de sos de Crabile of Arzana had been shot while attempting to

130

desert. He said he had heard of a sergeant asking for a permit for a firing squad and that Stocchino from Arzana was involved in it. So they thought he was dead and had died a coward. But that in itself would scarcely matter, because the worst thing about it was that Manai threw a party to celebrate the death of "the coward". And another thing no-one wanted to let on to Samuele about was that they had told this story to Felice Stocchino on his deathbed . . .

And then Gonario had begun to drink, and men who have no self-control become like children; their mothers can do their best, but at a certain point a man should get himself together with a wife, as it ought to be. Now, Gonario was a handsome fellow and he worked like a horse, so why all this bother? Lonely as a leper, he was. "Look for a wife somewhere else," Antioca had told him one day, and he said: "I'm not ready yet!" But he started to drink, which means being at a point far worse than is generally thought.

All this happened while they thought Samuele was dead. And this was all the more reason not to tell him.

But this secret, which could be hidden about as easily as an illegitimate baby, lasted like a snowfall in March: barely a moment.

Three months went by, finding Samuele surrounded by the meagre comforts of a poor cottage, but at all events better off than in the trenches. To him the fire burning in the grate seemed a marvel, as did the chicory soup, and the horseradish fried in lard, and even the camp bed with its hard, compressed straw mattress. Antioca trembled whenever Samuele left the house. He was still in the obstinate habit of going about in uniform with his puttees, cloak, and even his peaked cap.

But when Samuele said he was going out, he did not mean he was going to the piazza. He would go to the very outskirts of town where he and Mariangela used to meet. All the time he had been away he had had no news of her, nor had he asked for any when he got home. All the same, and despite not knowing what to expect, he went every day to their trysting place at the same hour.

Genesia spoke to Antioca about Mariangela, and this was another thing they had not told Samuele: that her grandfather had sent her off to be a maid to a lawyer in Nuoro. But the women agreed that it was something they might tell him now.

When Samuele came home in a mood as black as a winter's morning, and the two of them were discussing how to broach the subject of Mariangela, Mariangela herself appeared in the doorway.

And that was an apparition indeed, I can assure you, such as to give anyone a fright, but one mingled with relief. Of the three secrets: the false news of Samuele's death, the lie they had told Felice on his deathbed and the departure of Mariangela for Nuoro, at least the last had been revealed and resolved. But that was no reason to stop worrying, far from it. The revelation of the third secret, in fact, brought with it the disclosure of the first. When Mariangela appeared in the doorway it was as if she were the one seeing a ghost. Samuele gave her a puzzled look, and she looked at him as if seeing a ghost and said so:

"They told us you were dead," she murmured.

Samuele looked round at the others. Genesia and Antioca lowered their eyes. At which Samuele saw the light. He understood that what matters is not the secret that is kept but the reasons for keeping it.

"Well, then," he said at last. "They gave me up for dead, so it means I'll live all the longer." But he said it with forced jollity.

That night Antioca could not sleep. Genesia, on the other hand, slept like the exhausted beast of burden that she was, while Gonario slept the deathlike sleep of the sot. As for

Samuele, he thought he slept a bit but he didn't. He thought he had understood something, but knew that it was not the truth. He therefore decided that at first light he would set off for Eʼlini and call on Redento Marras, a man he had always thought highly of.

Her family almost did not let Mariangela into the house, but then, to avoid a scandal, they allowed her in despite the fact that she had had the impudence to leave the employment of a gentleman in Nuoro, and a lawyer to boot. Yes, yes, a really respectable employer, says you, she answered with a tilt of her chin. She had become pretty bold since she had found Samuele again. She didn't give a damn.

"You'll come to a bad end," her father told her. "Yes, you'll come to a bad end!"

For the whole of 1919 things toddled along, neither very well nor very badly, and Samuele went into business with two other veterans from the Carso dealing and negotiating deals in livestock, and everything seemed to be going alright until a certain point . . . And that came when word began to spread that they weren't buying and selling, but rustling. So when four of Giovanni Bardi's animals went missing they jumped to the conclusion that Stocchino was a leopard who had not changed his spots. And they sent along the carabinieri. It was a clear sign that under the ashes of all those kisses and good wishes, beneath the fanfares and the rhetoric, the coals of prejudice were still glowing. And everywhere the whisper was that Manai, "the richest man in town", could not wait to lay hands on Samuele, whom he held guilty of the death of his son Battista even though he could not prove it. So they sent along the carabinieri with a specific charge, stating that on the night of 4–5 January, 1920, Samuele had been seen by witnesses crossing the Conc' 'e Mortu with four sheep belonging to Giovanni Bardi, son of Nicola. But they made a complete mess of everything, because all that night and the night before Samuele had been in bed with the pulmonary fever he'd had recurrently ever since Libya. He had the doctor's certificate and the prescription for the chemist. Manai had to send Bardi to apologise, cap in hand.

But the truce had been broken. We come to 15 January. War had taught Samuele a lesson or two, so he went on the attack. He put on his uniform so that everyone would know that the war – the real war – had broken out. The voice of the people, and that of God himself, began to cry out for vengeance and said that Stocchino was certainly not going to stomach this insult.

All the same, to see him in the street he seemed perfectly composed, talking to everyone and having a drink with them, telling everyone that working for Bardi, Manai, or even for Boi, was a risky business. When they asked him what on earth it had to do with Boi, Samuele simply shook his head. *He* very well knew what Emerenziano Boi had to do with it. There were debts both old and new to pay, and when you start to pay you pay the whole lot, he explained without explaining anything.

This is why everyone said that this was Stocchino's last year, because if he went on threatening Manai, Bardi and Boi he would never make it into 1921. No-one had forgotten the edict nailed to the church door five years earlier, and no-one for a moment supposed that the dead past would bury its dead. So the swarm of negotiators got busy again. Father Marci had a word with Antioca, Notary Porcedda had a word with Genesia . . . And even Redento Marras from Elìni, who had injured his foot working in the fields, sent word to Samuele that he had something to tell him. And this brings us to the 17th January.

At dawn on the 18th, when Samuele got out of bed to go to Redento Marras, he could not find his uniform.

Gonario, still half-seas over, had put it on to play the fool in the village. Once a boozing shepherd, now just a drunk, he was taken advantage of by everyone because he was so vulnerable. Shrewd enough, but not intelligent, Gonario knew a lot about the land and livestock, but understood little or nothing about men and women. So, now that he had no sheep to look after he had become a mere derelict, and a pathetic one at that. It was Antioca more than anyone who grieved over this: that such a generous heart should have come to rely on the compassion of others.

But dressed up as he was in Samuele's uniform, with the grey-green cloak and cap, Gonario thought he had really become a man again because, as Antioca kept on saying, not even a drunkard wants to be a drunkard. Not even he himself wanted it. There in the piazza someone stared at him and he was tremendously bucked, because for once someone had looked at him without commiserating. Or so it seemed to him. So on he went as happy as Larry, thinking he was almost like Samuele. Until he came to Tanino Moro's house. Tanino saw him all got up like that and thought: let's go to the farm and play a joke on Peppeddu. Peppeddu was his hireling shepherd, and had always had a mortal fear of uniforms. So off they went towards the Manna estate where Tanino had a small olive grove, a few fruit trees, a small sheep pen and a pigsty.

Back at home Samuele had been raising all hell. He thought at first that the women had taken his uniform to wash it, but he only had to look around to see that Gonario's own clothes were all piled on a chair near his bed . . . Therefore in mufti, in clothes which had grown quite strange to him, Samuele sallied forth to find his brother. In the piazza they told him that Gonario was wearing his uniform and was swanking around, but they had no idea where he had gone or with whom. But at that moment he met Tanino Moro racing in on horseback with a face as white as a sheet. And all he could babble was Gonario, Gonario, Gonario . . .

*

They buried Gonario at dawn on 20 January, 1920. They had taken off the uniform, even though when it comes down to it he was the only war victim in the Stocchino family. He had waged war against himself, against his wretched existence, against the consequences of a hostility there was no way of placating, but which grew and flourished more than ever. The last shovelful of soil that covered Gonario's grave amounted to a solemn oath. Everyone said they could not understand what had happened, but Samuele knew very well. He was one of those who don't take long to cotton on to things. And now, his thoughts locked within him as in a safe, he made himself the speech of a lifetime. My enemies are powerful, he told himself, but they have made two mistakes: the first mistake was to declare war on me, and the second was not to realise that it wasn't me inside that uniform. It was as clear as daylight: whoever killed Gonario had got the wrong person. Like Luigi Crisponi in his vision. He too had mistaken Gonario for Samuele. He too had mistaken the identity.

Gonario was buried in the morning and first thing in the afternoon Samuele was on his way to Elìni.

Redento Marras, unable to rise from his chair, held out his arms towards him with tears in his eyes. He implored him not to do what everyone was saying he would do. But Samuele, having learned to take death in his stride but to be unbending in vengeance, did not even answer. He knew Redento was saying that because as a godfather he was bound to, because there was holy oil between them, so it was his duty to calm troubled waters. All the same, he did not manage to look convinced. Insomuch that Redento was scared:

"Remember, those people don't get things wrong twice."

"But they have got things wrong. They've got everything wrong . . . And now I must be going, it's getting late."

Redento watched him go.

V

In which we show how everything is unfailingly repeated

It was cold on the night of Saint Sebastian, martyr to the Faith, bound to a pillar and pierced by the arrows of the emperor's archers. Samuele's father Felice, a lifetime before, had told him that justice lives in the houses of the rich and that the faith of black bread, of simple people, is nothing but a forgotten tale.

Sergeant Stocchino came by moonlight to the house of Emerenziano Boi. There, at that spot and faced with that recurrence, he realised a terrible thing: that the beginning of all this had not been the bungle in the potato field. No, it had started with the refusal of a glass of water. Simply that. And it had not been the act in itself, but the manner of it. That brutal transgression against the unwritten laws of basic human solidarity. So it had been, and such as to leave no doubt as to what a solitude, what a tremendous, desperate, irredeemable solitude one can plunge into. Samuele realised that from that night onwards, everything that happened had been only one step further towards the abyss. He knew in his heart of hearts that that night had forever put paid to any possibility of redemption.

The full moon was about to sink beneath the skyline jagged as the edge of a broken eggshell, a moon slothful with an almost deathlike sloth, as if already in its first sleep.

Who knows how long Samuele prowled round and round Emerenziano Boi's silent house? He himself would be the last person to know. It may have been minutes or it may have been hours. The twentieth of January, 1920. Saint Sebastian, transfixed with arrows. But it is not so hard to understand how desperately he sought to give a name to what he thought he had to do . . . What he thought was the only solution to everything: to start again from the beginning. To put a topsy-turvy world the right way up again . . .

All of a sudden I remembered the look in my father's eyes and in that look I saw that I had to do what I did . . . I'm not happy about it, not happy at all, but you can't explain these things. Every time I think about it I tell myself I was a real fool, just a stupid fool to wreck my life like that. But it's not as if a man is alone in doing things – he thinks he's making a decision while all the time he's not deciding a bloody thing. Do you think I wouldn't have chosen a different kind of life?

Now he can never go back home again. This he knows, but that is the way of things.

So Stocchino was now a multiple murderer on the run. "Murder in Ogliastra!" cried the newspapers; adding "barbarous misdeed", "slaughter", "massacre", and so on.

It may seem incredible, but now that he was an outlaw with a big price on his head he gained in people's respect. Manai thought twice about laughing at "the sergeant". So did his crony Bardi. But they also thought that his being outlawed meant safety and protection for them.

"It would be worth our while to give him a helping hand when occasion arises," said Manai, before him a dish of lamb stuffed with wild fennel. "Yes, yes," he nodded, "Then when the moment comes, we'll get him."

And in fact Samuele Stocchino the bandit received nothing but signs of warm sympathy from Manai and Bardi. Help for the family and social respect.

Samuele seemed willing enough to accept all this. Things were working out as if his being on the run could eventually restore him to normal life. He had been a dangerous hero and now he was a murderer on the run. And such a person, it must be understood, has a meaning, a history and even a literature. Inside that particular clod of earth all the seeds must be those of familiar plants, of which the names are known.

Manai, being older and wiser, the possessor of ancient wisdom, thought that Stocchino on the run was less of a danger to him than Stocchino the hero. This was because in his world it was known since time immemorial that for outlaws there were rules, but for heroes there were none.

But Manai had never seen Samuele fight. Though older, wiser and the possessor of ancient wisdom, he did not understand that knowing the rules means the better to disobey them. So the second time Stocchino sat down to write, Manai could not believe what he was reading and quite lost his head . . .

All the servants and tenants of Giacomo Manai and his son Luigi will receive terrible wages at my hands.

I put my hand to this and remain
Samuele Stocchino

Ponziano Patteri, who found this message stuck into the gate of the Manai estate, almost had a heart attack. He arrived breathless at his employer's house and got him out of bed. "The richest man in town" took the message and held it close to his eyes to read better. Even more than the contents, it was the writing that struck fear into him: a pointed script, with curlicues and flourishes.

Giacomo Manai rushed into his son Luigi's bedroom without even knocking. The young man looked around him in befuddlement: "What's the time? What's happening?" Manai's only answer was to throw the letter onto the bed. It glided down onto Luigi's legs . . . And finally the script found speech: "Terrible wages . . ." muttered Manai to himself. Luigi was wide awake now.

"What are we to do?" he asked.

Manai slumped into a chair. "I know what we'll do," he said.

PART FOUR

Triumph, Danse Macabre and Other Liturgies of Death

A dense steam scalds my demented heart:
It bubbles fiercely in the depths, in the marrow of my bones,
Running through my veins . . .

Seneca the Younger, Phaedra

Chorus

Hanged. Don't ask the hanged man what he did. Just hanged. The split second before the answer comes. Here there is no tragedy to tell of, simply a return to the beginning. Hanged. Air is a good support, for with its conflicting currents it produces stability. The stillness of the hanging body. Tightening and choked breath, as at the bottom of the drop. Don't ask the hanged man what he did. He will tell you he's been hanged for a dream that went wrong, for a deed that went awry, for the woman he loved. He'll say that at that moment he is reading Villon along with the crows. He'll say that his shrivelled eye socket still retains some dreams in its shreds of flesh. That hanging body is waiting to dance, to sway just a little, when God's breath arrives through the open window. Have pity on that body; respect that last glimpse of the light. On his withering skin lies the mystery of a hieroglyphic dream. Like the bottom of a dried-out lake. Don't ask the dancer to explain his steps. He will say he can't explain how he does it. Or, rather, that he can't put it into words. That all that twisting and elasticity comes from within him, from the everyday breath of life, from some overmastering spirit. Hanged. Don't ask the hanged corpse to tell you his fate. He would tell you of a painter, a madman, a secret. He would tell you of the frenzy of truth that is only too true, like a photograph. And then silence, with all his thoughts positioned to make some sense, like the fibres of a piece of cord that defies the greed of gravity. Like the strands of a rope. Like a plummet lancing through the night of the depths. Cold light, rigour of exactitude. Mad glimmer of a dying body. Ask no more of him. Ask him not what he did. He has been waiting there in prayer, a mummy throughout the ages. Since they used to sing to the moon. And he knew the silent death throes of immortality. Ask him not what he did.

I

First Book of the Dead: Battista, Felice, Gonario

Battista Manai

Battista Manai was killed by his own stupidity, he was less a thief than a child, a dunce. He died in 1915, or thereabouts. They then started saying that he'd been killed by the bandit Stocchino because he had tried to seduce his fiancée. But it's not as if anyone ever knew who had really killed him . . . If Battista had not been the son of "the richest man in town" he'd have come to a sticky end a lot sooner. Because he was a block-head and high-handed to boot, and his father had spent more time getting him out of trouble than resting easy in his mind. In fact it was whispered in the village that it wasn't so unlikely, knowing old man Manai, that he himself had paid a hired worker to get rid of that troll of a son. And then there was the matter of Mariangela Palimodde, who as everybody knew was in love with Samuele Stocchino. So whether or not it was Samuele Stocchino who killed Battista Manai, it could not really be said that he had given great offence to his father, Giacomo. In fact, if that was the way things were, he had done him a favour. In short, what happened was that Battista Manai, as usual, was putting on a show of working by handing out orders right and left to hired shepherds, who had orders not to obey his orders. He was one of those who does more harm than good. All he had been told was that it was time for him to settle down and find a good woman to look after him. Then they told them that they had found one. Then they told him that his aunt the nun and his elder sister were negotiating with the family of the girl they had chosen. There are many different accounts of Battista's death. Some say he was beaten to death by robbers; others that he had been drinking and had fallen over and cracked his skull; others still said, as above, that a Manai servant had been paid to do it; and finally there was the legend of Samuele Stocchino. This story tells that Samuele was lurking near the gate of his farm, stabbed him in the heart and then, so the story goes, cut out his heart and took it home to have it served up to him with onions and vinegar. The carabinieri came to the conclusion that there was no proof of anything. Stocchino came out of it clean, and a week later he left for the front line. Therefore, either the carabinieri decided that it wasn't worth depriving the war effort of a useful man, or else it was in fact Manai himself who had hushed the whole thing up.

Felice Stocchino

. . . And this is linked to the death of Felice Stocchino. In fact the word was that Felice had died of fright. He had been out looking for wild chicory and asparagus when one of the Manai clan came and told him that his son might have avoided the hand of the law, but he would not avoid the vengeance of "the richest man in town", who was going to make him pay for Battista's death. Felice told him that Samuele had nothing to do with Battista's death. The other said that not only was he guilty of it but he, Felice, had better get his black armband ready because Samuele would not return from the war alive, because if the Austrians didn't kill him someone else would see to it and he hoped he had made himself clear. This terrified Felice, because if they had gone so far as to pay someone in the army to bump off Samuele it seemed even worse than the war itself. It was as if his son had enemies wherever you looked; as if he was never safe. So he went home chewing over the matter of a hired killer in the trenches, and realised how small and how utterly powerless he was. What could he do in the great history of the outside world? What indeed! If he had known how to write he could have warned Samuele, but he could not write and nor could he trust a third party. And what if they had not meant it seriously and he got Samuele all worked up for nothing? And again, what if the man who told him had meant it in a friendly way, so that it really would be better to warn Samuele? All this while he made his way home. Antioca saw him come in looking like a ghost, asked him what was the matter and he said it was nothing, he just wasn't feeling very well, so maybe he'd put his feet up and then lie down for a while. Antioca left him just about to get up from his chair. She had things to do in the yard. Meanwhile Genesia came into the kitchen to fetch a clean, ironed apron and saw her father bent over as if he wanted to get to his feet but had not managed it, so had decided to stay put. She went to him and he peered at her before even recognising her. "Oh dear," he muttered. "Oh, dear girl . . ." Genesia asked what was up, but instead of answering he asked what should be done about Samuele on account of what he had just been told. Genesia asked what it was and who had told him. But Felice made no answer. So Genesia knew something was wrong and became worried. Felice managed a sort of smile and asked her to help him stand up. But as she started to do so, she realised she was lifting a dead weight. By the time they called the doctor Felice had not been breathing for at least a quarter of an hour. Genesia ran off to tell the notary, because they had guests for lunch and were expecting her. As for Gonario, who knows where he had gone drinking . . . Antioca wept alone. Then Father Marci arrived and said that they must tell Samuele. Antioca was not sure if it was a good thing or not, the poor boy was in hell and it was better not to upset him; the important thing was that Felice had made a good end and

147

without any suffering. But Father Marci insisted that in any case they must let Samuele know, perhaps he might get compassionate leave, even if with all the trouble at the front leave had been suspended. He said he would see to it, just write a simple letter without worrying Samuele . . .

That night, while they were keeping vigil, Genesia told Antioca what Felice had said just before he died. Antioca could not make head or tail of it. To her he had said nothing, except that he was tired and wanted to go and lie down. The two women exchanged glances, then shook their heads as if to say that it was useless to fret over the unfathomable mysteries of the dying. "Goodness knows what he meant," Genesia concluded, and they fell silent . . . But during the wake the two of them talked about the time Giacobbe Muntoni, God rest his soul, just before he died, asked them to move the ladder from the bed. What ladder? They asked. But he was already more on that side than this: a ladder that only he saw, in fact. On another occasion Luisedda Piras was staring fixedly at a corner of the ceiling and her daughter asked her what she was looking at. But she went on staring, and seemed even a little offended, giving no answer except babbling a few incomprehensible sounds with her parched lips . . . Which all goes to show that the dying know where they are going, even if we don't . . .

Gonario Stocchino

Then it was Gonario's turn. And here matters get more complicated and serious because there are so many rumours. It is certain that he was tricked, there's no point in denying that. Gonario Stocchino was a bit slow on the uptake. Gonario was as simple-minded as Samuele was sharp, but he was by no means stupid. That not. In fact he had a sort of astuteness of his own; he could tell jokes and he was good company. But he didn't have the stuffing, as they used to say. Heavens alive, for guzzling and swilling in the tavern he was perfect company. He was perfect also for dealing with livestock and working like a horse. But for anything else he didn't have the right stuff. He was truly affectionate, but he lacked the fire that Samuele had all too much of. Every time he made a business deal he lost more than he earned. Antioca kept that son of hers close to her skirts because she had to. She wasn't easy in her mind unless he was out in the country, because the countryside was Gonario's natural element. There he became a different person, one who knew things that ordinary folks are not privileged to know. He was sought after by all the landowners around for the wonderful skill with which he tended their vines and grafted olive trees . . . He had enormous, coarse hands, with huge fingers and horny palms, but he could stroke animals so gently as to tame them in a trice. He was as natural as a breeze ruffling a sheep's wool, the bristles of a pig or a horse's mane. They drew breath together, did Gonario and his animals, they sheltered from the fierce sun under the same oak tree. As in the ancient of days, when men and beasts contributed to the grandeur of creation, without saints or altars, but life and life only, that lasts as long as it lasts. Gonario knew that knowing things can be a curse. He was a creature of nature even when he drank himself into a stupor. As when the long-entreated rain becomes a destructive cloudburst, as when a sunny day becomes the very forge of Vulcan, or a promising, delicate bud is trampled by a boar. That was the way he drank, like any of those things of nature which suddenly lose their sense of proportion.

When, on the morning of his death, he was wearing Samuele's uniform, he had all the lucid determination of those about to die. Who could tell whether he would return from where he wanted to go? He could not tell, he could no longer tell, because his punishment was the absence of desire, just as he had always wanted it. And now, a shell of his former self,

149

he was going around in Samuele's uniform. So he was no longer Gonario. Wearing that uniform, in fact, he was seized by the same feverish determination his brother had always had. It was when wearing those clothes that a bullet through the neck fired from behind the wall of Tanino Moro's pigsty cut off his life. Like a flash of lightning cleaving a tree trunk.

II

*In which we speak of how ancient wisdom can
put a flea in your ear*

And now it is that Death begins to feast. Two of Manai's hired
shepherds, driving a hundred and seventy sheep towards
Orgosolo, were found dead, the flock dispersed. Bardi lost three
hectares of olive grove, devoured by a raging fire by night . . . The
Boi house had become home to wild boar and other animals.
Domo rutta. Arzana was wearing mourning armbands. Stocchino
was still around, bright as the sun and just as cocksure. You'd
find him chatting at the crossroads, offering drinks and accept-
ing offers. Then, perhaps that very evening, word got around
that one of Bardi's workers had decided it wasn't worth risking
his life for a crust of bread, and went and told his boss that
Stocchino hadn't minced his words: *All the servants and tenants
of Giacomo Manai and his son Luigi will receive terrible wages at my
hands. I put my hand to this and remain Samuele Stocchino.* And
such wages would not feed his children; it would make orphans
of them. So no-one wanted to work in their fields anymore, and
when workers were brought in from outside, they didn't take
long to realise how the land lay and packed their bags.

To Sergeant Palmas it looked like a case of criminal use of
threat, but that would merely be one more charge to be brought
against that animal Stocchino, who already had the killing in
the Boi house to answer for.

Everyone's hands were tied by the lack of evidence. Manai
no longer dared leave his house, but he'd be damned if he'd

give that vile dog Stocchino the pleasure of seeing him leave Arzana. "Us, needing the protection of the law!" thundered the old man. Just imagine, to be so mortified by such a scoundrel!

The only good thing for Samuele was his meetings with Mariangela. They met on the sly, now even more often than before. They saw each other, but barely touched. With her he became a child again, hesitant, feeling inadequate. He felt unable even to speak, for he had only to look at her to feel he was bursting with unspoken happiness. Very like a pain. That was the only emotion he had felt since the time of their separation, of the abyss, of the loss of childhood.

It was sometimes difficult for them to meet, because Samuele had a price of ten thousand lire on his head. But he had found a good place, a large airy cave. And she would enter it as if it were a palace built especially as a home for their ill-starred love.

Mariangela would often watch Samuele sleeping. He felt safe only when he was with her and only with her did he let himself go. Sometimes he told her that when he was alone in the woods he could hear the trees breathing sighs, and hear the rocks trembling. In the populous night of his cave he had time to think about the way his life was heading. Every step a step towards the end. Every step a step towards the beginning. Everything he had gained had cost him all too much, but that was not what counted now: what counted was to pay them back in their own coin. The parched fields of Giacomo Manai and Giovanni Bardi were the outward signs of his own inner hell. The sepulchral silence to which he had reduced the whole village cried out his victory, but there in his cave, without Mariangela, Samuele was unable to sleep.

Too many breaths . . . I feel as if I were in the belly of the whale before it spat out Jonah. Too much darkness . . . as if I were on the

Corno Grande della Forca, lost in the night. Too alone, as on the point of death, when you are abandoned even by one who swore never to leave you, saying that the agreement lasts until death do you part, because as soon as one of you is heading towards the other side it's obvious that two of you can't go there, even if you die at the same moment, it's not that number that makes death: no number does. Death itself makes death. In war men died in heaps, but no-one died in company, they all died on their own. Too much death indeed, so I feel as if I'm living in the underworld.

Outside the cave sings the dawn, and rather than seeing it I hear it. I go out at night along with the owls and wild cats and ferrets. I know where a rat is by the scraping of its teeth on a walnut shell.

Then I can hear the steps of Mariangela: even without seeing her I know that she glances anxiously over her shoulder as she walks. Without seeing her I can count the steps that bring her to the mouth of the cave. And already I feel peace stroking the nape of my neck.

Those in the know swore that Mariangela died a virgin. They said that Mariangela did not yield herself even when she learned that she was going to die. But they also know the right time to speak. For the moment Mariangela was like the spouse of Jove himself with his thunderbolts. To so much as touch her was to ask to be struck by lightning, to invoke storm and tempest. She felt weary at times, and when her period approached she was always pale and exhausted. But her beauty was of that fundamental kind, a territory in which all beauties can flourish. Samuele himself did not know how that woman had come to have such a hold over him, but have it she did, oh yes! It was she who arranged things with her gentleness and ruled with her silence. He was a man who existed insofar as she did, and on the fatal day when he decided to disobey her

153

he became another person, but she did not cease to accept him. She was simply Mariangela. Mariangela Palimodde, aged thirty. She it was who kept him alive . . . She had rescued him from the abyss, and thereafter gave meaning to his return to life.

On 4 March, 1923, Antioca Leporeddu was arrested as an accessory. Such was the tenor of the times. News arrived from Cagliari that a bloodless revolution had swept through the nation. From the Ogliastra, from Barbagia, it was hard to tell what "nation" that was. However, it was from Rome that this revolution was due to arrive on the march. And arrive it did. A revolution of resolute, dark, energetic men who took the future into their own hands.

For three years now Giacomo Manai had been afraid to leave his house, going out only by day and surrounded by servants. And for three years Giovanni Bardi had been living in terror, growing so bloatedly fat that he looked double his former self. They lived on secret funds, put by in the good years, surreptitious assistance . . . Loans at exorbitant interest. Spurious sales.

Samuele did not have to do a thing. Or rather, it was enough to cut the hocks of a flock of sheep, set fire to a field, turn up at a drinking trough wearing his sergeant's cloak still stained with Gonario's blood. Or to cut the throat of a hireling still rash enough to be loyal to Samuele's enemies. The death of Emerenziano Boi and his family had left everyone incapable of reacting. After 20 January, 1920, things changed. Manai, who thought he understood all, realised that terrible times had disrupted all ways of speech, all possible words. He was old, there was no-one to succeed him, Samuele had won.

Then came the news from Cagliari and the veterans of the Carso were called upon to don the black shirt, invited to play the great game of "isms". So it was that Manai, more combatant than veteran, had himself made a black shirt, while another was made for Giovanni Bardi.

They travelled by night, pathetic figures hidden among a lorryload of sheep. Like two pitiful Ulysseses matched against a Polyphemus only one metre sixty-three tall. They arrived in Cagliari stinking of livestock in the best tradition of pelt-clad troglodytes. His Excellency Gandolfo Asclepia, Prefect of Cagliari, received them as the dwarf king received the shepherd king of Montenegro: with barely concealed contempt. It was a gloomy carnival of black shirts, of promises and prospects: it would not be long before even the interior of Sardinia had a prefect. It was a celebration of possible futures, of a great nationwide party that would satisfy the just demands of regions which had contributed so much to the glorious war effort.

All their words were far too high and mighty for the story which Manai had to tell. And too small for his expectations.

His enemies in Cagliari, and Stocchino preening himself in the piazza.

"Who is Stocchino?" asked the prefect, already afflicted by pangs of hunger.

"A sergeant decorated in the war," explained Manai, whose ancient wisdom advised him to choose the right moment to put a flea in someone's ear.

And in fact the prefect's face darkened a little. "A war hero?"

Manai nodded. "And what a hero, Your Excellency . . ."

The prefect rang the bell on his desk. Giovanni Bardi opened his eyes with a start. The office door flew open and in came a skinny little man with a moustache. He was about to speak when the prefect forestalled him. "What do we know about this sergeant . . . ?" He broke off and glanced at Manai.

"Stocchino," supplied the latter. "Stocchino."

So it came about that on 4 March, 1923, the carabinieri put the cuffs on Antioca Leporeddu. Mariangela had almost made up her mind not to tell Samuele when she found that he already knew. She could tell by the look in his eyes. By this time looks were enough for them to understand each other. But never an expression such as she now saw on Samuele's face. Go on home, this isn't the day for it, said he with a flicker of his eyelids. She yearned to embrace him, but she knew she had to go.

III

Second Book of the Dead: Nicolina Bardi,
Ponzieri Patteri, Luigi Manai

That night died Nicolina Bardi. Antioca was in jail, staring at a cup of hot milk with Lance-Corporal Butto watching over her without daring to say a word.

"If you're expecting Samuele here, you've made a mistake," she said without turning her head.

The policeman shrugged. He didn't really understand this business of arresting relations so as to lay hands on fugitives, but it had always been that way.

After an hour or so Father Marci appeared. He sat facing Antioca and began to speak softly to her . . . Word had it that Manai in person was doing his best to get her out of prison. Manai and no other! Antioca did not believe it for a moment. Or rather, concluded that Manai didn't give a damn about her but was trying to ingratiate himself with Samuele, the crafty bastard . . .

"But if Samuele only knew how his chosen way of life is hurting you . . ."

"He knows it, he knows it, Father, but he also knows the great wrong that's been done to us. What do you want of me?"

"I'd like you to send a message to Samuele."

Antioca gave him a long look, then took a sip of her steaming milk.

"As things are going at the moment, a war hero would have a chance of starting again in life."

Antioca's eyes lit up as if she were awaiting a friendly nod from the Madonna.

That same night, just as Antioca was talking to Father Marci, death came to Nicolina Bardi. The blind rage of Samuele was like the hand of a housewife smoothing out a counterpane: his mother was in chains, blighted by the law, and he was out there lapping up the night-time. Eager to kill. Lapping up the night-time, as smooth as a well-made bed; and he had even taken off his uniform and shaved. As glowing as a new bridegroom, he was, but glowing with the lust for blood.

The woman was walking very quickly, without steadying the basket of flat bread on her head. She was late, having spent the whole day kneading enough bread to last through the hard times to come. And now she was hurrying. When Samuele appeared before her she did not recognise him, but he recognised her. Nicolina was a simple soul, with all the modesty of a third-born.

Then the night enveloped all and everyone. Samuele had taken that alleyway to try to shake off his seething rage. He knew they would not harm Antioca, but the affront was great: to take an elderly woman and make her sleep the cold sleep behind bars was an act of pure malice.

Nicolina told herself that the dark alley was a short cut and she was too tired to think straight.

So it was that they met. She saw the young man at the end of the alley and speeded up, while he slowed down. They were all but submerged in darkness. Their intentions were clean contrary: she had no wish to see who it was before her, while he could scarcely believe he had come across the woman he thought he recognised. She was telling herself that she had been unwise in wanting to get home at all costs, when she could have stayed overnight with her neighbour.

Just as Father Marci, seated opposite Antioca in prison, was

158

mentioning a possible agreement, a shaft of light from a window fell across the alley. Eyes met. It took Nicolina only a second to realise that that smiling young man was nothing less than a nightmare in flesh and blood. She was a simple soul, but she knew at once that to be a Bardi face to face with a Stocchino, when the law had just made a public example of Antioca, could only mean one thing. So she dropped her basket of bread in the gutter and opened her mouth to cry Help, that she was a dead woman, that the devil had come to fetch her off.

They could not know that their meeting was mere chance, but they had enough millennia of belief behind them to know there is no such thing as chance. At some point one of the Fates had to snap the thread.

Samuele drew his knife and put on his smile, because that woman was a kind of response, like a mouse for a cat, a tooth for a tooth. Whoever had the task of watching over her star-crossed life was asleep on the job . . .

The point of the knife entered just enough to cause her pulsing carotid artery to burst. The gush of blood surprised her, with lips not yet ready to receive it. She opened her mouth wide, savouring its rich, rusty taste. The taste of night, Samuele would have said.

She clutched at Samuele's shoulders in a last desperate grasp at life, then her arms fell to her sides as her breath came shorter and shorter. As for him, he just smiled at her, as if he could see the breath leaving that wounded body. As if he saw it in the form of an angel fleeing, wafting its ethereal wings to leave that fleshly dwelling forever.

Nicolina fell face down, and the drain in the middle of the alley carried away her blood and her last breath. Samuele watched her die and was as happy as a foul deed can make one. Now he would sleep, for his rage seemed to have seeped away with Nicolina's life. Yes, he would like to sleep, but he still had work to do.

In the yard of the Bardi house there was a chestnut tree, plumb there in the middle of the courtyard walled about like a fortress. The tips of the longest branches brushed the unscalable wall. Beside the doorway there was a granite bench. It was there that the family used to sit before the quarrels began, and it was there that the women would sit and chuckle in the cool of the summer evenings. It was on that very bench that Samuele placed the letter which he had written, putting a stone on it as a paperweight.

> *To the people of Arzana and all neighbouring townships because they are saying that I am a scoundrel whereas I am a reasonable person and wish no harm to anyone who does not deserve it. Therefore, whoever collaborates or aids my adversaries Giovanni Bardi and Giacomo Manai along with his rotten son Luigi will be paid by me in their own coin.*
>
> *I sign myself as ever,*
> *Samuele Stocchino*

Ah, it was the terrible law of death that calls for another death. It was almost daybreak when Samuele, utterly exhausted, regained his cave deep in the hillside, the lair of a hunted beast.

At that very moment Antioca was being taken home by two terrified recruits. Genesia was there to receive her, ashen-faced and distraught with care.

At that moment also the cry of Giovanni Bardi, shown the corpse of his slaughtered daughter, cleft the night.

Mariangela was wakened by fearful abdominal pains.

Next morning Manai, since Nicolina had been his niece, dared the light of day to pay a visit to his mourning brother-in-law. However, the main reason was that the contents of Samuele's letter had passed from mouth to mouth, and he wanted to see it with his own eyes. He had lain awake racking his brains all night long and thought he had found a solution. And this solution was to stop being on the defensive and go on the attack. Therefore Ponziano Patteri, representing "the richest man in town", had already set out for Elìni. He was to visit Redento Marras, who had bonds of the holy oil with the Stocchino family.

But now, in daylight, accompanied only by his son Luigi, here was Giacomo Manai knocking at the door of Giovanni Bardi. Without a glance to right or left he stalked straight through the candle-lit room where the women were praying over poor, meek Nicolina.

Red-eyed, Giovanni Bardi followed him into the kitchen.

"Pull yourself together," snapped Manai, grasping the Stocchino letter in trembling hands. "Stop blubbering, because the time has come to make him pay for it."

Bardi looked at the old man in bewilderment, although what he had said was perfectly simple. What perplexed him, all the same, was the idea that his dead daughter had not been enough to break the camel's back, but that letter was. It had to be explained to the broken-hearted father that in the personal universe of Giacomo Manai the family was a mere satellite, whereas his property was the planet. Giovanni Bardi had a moment of hesitation, but then he paid attention.

"This is our next step," Manai was saying.

Night was already falling when Ponziano Patteri reached Elìni. Redento Marras welcomed him and gave him broad beans and bacon fat with barley bread. Patteri ate without a word, emptying the plate and gulping down the rough wine. He knocked back the last mouthful and wiped his lips.

"Redé," he started in. "Things can't go on like this."

Redento Marras made no move. In the archway was the

touchstone, in the field was the pen to shelter the sheep, in the earth was the root that drew in the water, in the river was the estuary which flowed out into the sea.

Yet he made no movement. He had no reply for Ponziano Patteri, envoy of Manai. It was a story that had no solution. No point in talking about it because it was like talking about an abyss, a precipice.

"There's nothing I can do. Nothing," said Redento Marras.

"Get him to come here," suggested Patteri. "We'll get them to meet here at your place and see if we can patch things up. Everyone trusts you. We'll get them face to face and have them talk man to man, each with his own point of view . . ."

"Not here," interjected Marras. "At Sa Muddizzi."

"At Sa Muddizzi be it," said Patteri.

We come to 14 May, 1923. For two weeks Patteri and Marras have been at work to arrange the meeting. Everything has been thought of: that Manai is willing to come to an agreement and so is Bardi; that Samuele demands the name of whoever killed his brother Gonario; that the authorities in Cagliari are offering very good terms to decorated veterans; that Manai and Bardi are willing to have a collection for the sum of twenty thousand lire, the price on Samuele's head. And thus put an end to the quarrel.

Sa Muddizzi is a lonely farmhouse lying on the eastern slopes of the hill, a landscape barren but with good grazing land.

Samuele got dressed early, when it was still dark. From the heart of the wood came the sound of human footsteps. A sound that Samuele recognised more than any other. This was not the hesitant step of Mariangela, nor the firm step of a hunter, nor the cautious footstep of the soldier. But it was that of a man, as he could tell from the brittle sound of the crunching leaves. So, moving through that terrain which he knew like the back of his hand, he came up behind the man. When he seized him round the neck the unknown sounded almost thankful.

"It's me!" he croaked as he smothered a cry.

Samuele looked him in the face, realised he knew that face well but could not remember where he had seen it.

"I'm Rubanu. Rubanu from Ulassai."

No, he had not forgotten that Samuele had saved his life when he was within inches of facing a firing squad. So he had decided to do what he was doing now: to warn him. Samuele did not know that four days earlier the carabinieri had arrested Redento Marras, or that Ponziano Patteri, as drunk as a fish, had let it slip that at the meeting at Sa Muddizzi Samuele would meet nothing but a hail of lead. He did not know that since Manai and Bardi had donned the black shirt they could count on support from very high up, from Cagliari itself. He did not know how things had changed, because things changed a little bit every day. Samuele listened. Rubanu looked him in the face and failed to understand how the destiny of the great man he saw before him had played him such tricks as to turn him into a hunted beast.

Despite this, Samuele did go to Sa Muddizzi. Rubanu had a hard time keeping up with him. Some way before they got there Samuele told Rubanu to stop right where he was. Rubanu replied that he had come this far and might as well go the whole hog. He owed him too much, he said, and he was handy with a gun.

"That's why you have to wait," explained Samuele. "They may be expecting me, but not both of us. If they see us together they'll be on their guard." Rubanu said he'd keep him covered. Samuele therefore went on alone. Only a yard or two from the drystone wall Ponziano Patteri came out to meet him.

"Where's Redento Marras?" enquired Samuele.

Patteri was wrong-footed. "We're waiting for him too," he said, "but he hasn't shown up yet."

Samuele drew a deep breath as if to give an answer, but instead from beneath his uniform cloak he drew his gun and shot the man point-blank full in the chest. Ponziano Patteri threw out his arms as if to take flight; and indeed he did fly back as the blast of lead carried him off as a leaf on the wind. He fell to the ground with a thump, with the fixed stare of one with no time to realise what has happened.

From behind the wall came a hail of bullets, and then more and more of them . . . Luigi Manai brandished his gun and yelled, "You swine . . . Fix that son of a whore!"

Samuele felt a bullet sear his side like a whiplash. He bent double, gasping, but the Manai clan were now firing ten to a dozen. It was a storm of fire. Samuele held up a hand as if to tell them to stop firing: a bullet went straight through his palm. Then he crouched down and set off running through the underbrush, but he had not taken two strides before he realised he was dragging one leg. Luigi Manai and his men pursued him, urging each other on as they smelled the blood of the hunted quarry and the end of all their troubles. Rubanu heard the shots in the distance and began to run: could that fox of a Samuele be drawing the pack of hounds towards him? So he went forward to meet them.

But it wasn't that way at all. Samuele, panting his heart out and scarcely able to see, realised that his decision to face up to a hazardous challenge concealed a wish that it would all soon be over. The mere idea of being near the end made him run all the more. On the other hand Manai's men were running because they knew that once Stocchino reached the thick of the forest it would be impossible to ferret him out. But they did not know that by now Samuele thought only of rendering the inevitable more difficult. So he ran, not even knowing how. He ran.

He simply ran.

That morning Mariangela got up feeling very sick. She had taken only a few steps into the room before she felt something

164

oozing down between her thighs. It was warm and gelatinous. Automatically she wiped it with the hem of her nightshirt. The material was stained a dark red, but it was not menstrual, more like clotted blood. For four days she had been in bed with this awful feeling of weakness. For four days she had had no word from Samuele. When she called for help she did not even realise she had collapsed on the floor.

On he ran . . . Luigi Manai had the look of a man whose whole life and future depended on this moment. Rather than seeing him, he caught the scent of Stocchino as he fled doubled up among the mastic shrubs. He loosed off an occasional shot towards the fugitive's shadow, but someone behind him shouted to him not to waste ammunition.

It occurred to Samuele that for four days there had been no sign of Mariangela.

Rubanu looked round him in bewilderment. Now that the undergrowth was denser his fear was that the shots would rebound off protruding rocks. He heard a lot of shouting in front of him: they were saying not to waste ammunition. They said Stocchino was walking into a trap.

And indeed they knew it well, because Samuele's flight ended at the edge of the abyss. A narrow chasm which he recognised at once; he had spent four days in it when he was seven years old.

Now they were face to face, Luigi Manai and Samuele Stocchino. Manai's lips were trembling; he could not believe that he had caught Stocchino, that he was able to speak to him at such close quarters. Samuele felt the abyss tickling his heels.

"Now I'm going to shoot you," Luigi Manai was stuttering, his whole frame quaking with terror. His eyes had the crazed look of a man about to have a stroke, and as he stuttered, "I'll

165

kill you, I'll kill you," his voice was strangled to a whisper. Samuele eyed him steadily, thought of the void yawning behind him, and moved one foot an inch or so backwards. If he took a half step back there'd be no ground beneath his feet.

Manai's retainers were all yelling at him to shoot, for God's sake! But Luigi's lips were drawn back in a fixed grimace. He felt his blood running cold, and felt Stocchino's eyes looking through and beyond him. In these few seconds when they were face to face Luigi put his life on the line.

"You're a dead man," he yelled once more. But it was once too often.

The shot rang out, but the gun was Samuele's, concealed beneath his sergeant's cloak. Luigi could not have grasped that: he had never been to war. Before Luigi's men had realised that their master had been blasted out of existence and they had to shoot back, Samuele had stepped back into the abyss.

Stupefied, they scanned the depths. There was no sign of Samuele's body.

The doctor's eyes told all. But when he turned to Mariangela, he smiled with his mouth. That was how she knew, without a shadow of doubt, that her days were numbered.

Back in the village Manai's men were broadcasting the war news. Ponziano Patteri and Luigi Manai were trundled around on a cart like two wild boar ready for a banquet. Samuele was dead.

Rubanu ran till his lungs were bursting to the edge of the precipice and peered down. Mother of God . . . ! Holy Mother of God, something was moving on the branches of a big juniper tree rooted in the rock face.

166

IV

The third burial and resurrection of Samuele

"Where am I?"

"Safe," said Rubanu. "Strike me dead if you aren't."

Samuele opened his eyes. Rubanu felt as if he were witnessing something he could never even describe. Only he knew what it had cost him to haul Samuele out of that that crevasse. The bed was comfortable, but Rubanu lived in a sort of hovel in the wilds around Ulassai.

"How long have I been here?" asked Samuele.

Twelve days and still no news. Antioca had given up hoping. So she told herself that the time had come to close her eyes forever. Still as beautiful as when she used to walk in the procession of the Immaculate Conception, she sat in the chair that had been Felice's chair and had always been there beside the fireplace. But first, taken by a sudden thought, she went to the chest, opened it and rummaged among the best towels in search of Samuele's heart, the broken pebble which she had tied back together with string. She grasped it tightly in her fist. Then, making her way back to the chair in which Felice had died, she went to die herself.

Mariangela was better now; a little colour had even crept back into her cheeks. So she started walking, knowing well that the rumour of Samuele's death was not true. It had never been true. There is no death without a dead body. So she started walking because she knew that wherever he was he would come back, and when he came back he would want to find her beside him. At the cave there was no sign of life.

Samuele looked at the ostrich returning his gaze from Rubanu's book of animal pictures. It was like a sea monster, but on land. That's how it was.

He tried to rise and managed to sit up. "Twelve days," said Rubanu. Samuele looked at his bandaged hand. His painful ribs were bandaged too. "Not even hell will let you in, Sergeant."

Outside, summer was seething. The gentians were preparing their July blooms.

Silence.

When Samuele got back to the cave he felt that he was not alone. His wounds were aching and he had brought along the animal book Rubanu had given him.

There on the bed Mariangela seemed to be sleeping, but Samuele recognised death at once. So he lay down beside her and thought that when he died he would like it to be here where she had died. The lucid calm with which he understood he had lost everything frightened him a little. But above all he was frightened by all the life that lay before him.

Rumours, rumours everywhere

I saw Stocchino when everyone was saying he was dead, and the Manai and Bardi clans and all their friends had paid for a Mass and a new processional robe for the Madonna, embroidered by the nuns, as well as jewels and a crown of solid silver. Anyway, there they all were in church, giving thanks. I was digging my vegetable patch and I saw him plain as daylight. Looking older, and saddened . . . yes, I'm sure he was sad.

At any rate, there he went across the piazza in his torn, grubby uniform and stationed himself outside the church door. Well, you should have heard the screams when someone in there said that Stocchino was outside. They barred the door at once, while Stocchino just stood there calmly looking at the closed door. Then he traced the letter "S" on the ground with his foot and left just as he had come. Without anyone lifting a finger.

I had only just started working for Manai at the time they said Stocchino was dead. While he wasn't dead at all, far from it . . . We were all in church and then we were all going to have a meal together, when Mundinu came rushing in from the piazza trying to tell us something. Old Manai came close to hitting him in the face because he couldn't spit out what he had to say, but he just went on babbling away until someone made out the word "Stocchino". So everyone fell silent, even the altar boys. Even Father Marci, right in the middle of the *Gloria*. There was a terrible silence for a moment, then suddenly the women began to whimper and clutch their children to them. Some of them had not left the house for four years.

It was like when the Jews were making merry in the desert and adoring the golden calf, and they saw Moses coming down the mountain to spoil the party. The women gave their menfolk reproachful looks. The Dui, the Marcialis, the Secchi, all those families who had managed to keep out of the quarrel realised that by taking part in that service along with the Manai they had incautiously exposed and compromised themselves. But most of all they realised that from then on theirs was yet another name on the tiger's list . . .

And in fact before he left, standing in the middle of the piazza, Stocchino bellowed at the barred door of the church:

"I don't kill on the Lord's Day. There are six other days, so watch yourselves . . . I've seen you all, I know you all by name and you'd all better realise what to expect from me!"

By the time the carabinieri arrived there was no trace of him.

Just imagine how it was: that man had lost everything. He offered himself as a target, but the more he risked the more elusive he seemed. That aura of immortality was like a shield to him. All the time he was off the scene, being helped and nursed by Rubanu, the village had been enjoying all the elation and relief of waking from a nightmare. The men from the expedition to Sa Muddizzu had been bragging about a corpse they had never seen, but that perhaps they had willed themselves to see. Anyway, they thought that Stocchino would never emerge alive from the abyss into which he had plunged. So Manai had taken to strutting around in the piazza, and the townsfolk had started to be deferential again. All the more so because he was now wearing the black shirt and even there, in that last lost neck of the woods, the black shirt stood for something.

During the two months in which it was believed that Samuele was finally and incontrovertibly dead, a few farmhands began to cultivate the fields which had been abandoned for years, to prune olives already gone wild and to prop up rows of vines long since left to their own devices.

Those infants who had been born and grown to be toddlers in captivity now saw for the first time what the village looked like beyond their fortified courtyards. The liveliness of the women at market or at the public wash-trough was that of children seeing the world for the first time. Arzana put on white armbands, like a young bride.

But Samuele's reappearance put an end to all that. In fact it was the start of "The Terror". Now that all conventional decencies had been swept aside, that Antioca was in her unwept grave and Mariangela dead and lamented to the very last tear, Stocchino was fury incarnate.

Ancient wisdom knows this well, so that everyone who was in church on that Sunday in 1924 used every means to make it clear that they had nothing to do with the Manai or the Bardi clan. The very next day four people were found dead at the farm known as Mortu S'Omine where they were working in the main vineyard, quite oblivious of what had happened in the village the day before. Two of them were locals, but the other two were from the mainland, sent there by Mussolini to see if their own hunger could be assuaged by the hunger of others. The following Wednesday Bardi's daughter-in-law's first cousin was killed on the main road and so was Venerio Dui, whose mistake was to have been sitting in church three pews behind Giacomo Manai. The price on Samuele's head was raised to sixty thousand, but no-one was anxious to claim it.

Having now re-established the reign of terror, the only one he knew, Stocchino, maddened by loneliness, set his mind to the future. He had two brothers he did not even know, who since infancy had been farmed out to distant relations down around Oristano, and he had Genesia, who had left the notary and had gone to work as a maid for a doctor in Sassari, a whole world away.

The empty house had been left to rot and to the winds that blew, because the rightful owner did not have the heart, or perhaps the courage, to claim it.

So it was that they began to see him everywhere: in nunneries disguised as a nun, in woodland as naked as the First Man, at the water sources where he drank along with the animals, at the crossroads lying in wait for an enemy. They took to saying that if children could not sleep it was because the tiger was coming. Seven killings in 1925 alone. Always a hair's breadth from being caught, but always impossible to lay hands on.

Samuele was not a living person. Anyone who caught him would find that husk of nerves and muscles an empty shell. The few who had looked him in the eye had seen a bleak, distant look: that of a killer.

The know-alls said that a bunch of wealthy people in the area had taken advantage of the situation to curry favour with Stocchino and lay their hands on some of the property of his enemies. The know-alls said, Think it out for yourselves: would Stocchino have been able to do everything he has done all on his own?

But as the poet has it:

> *Como nessi no tenzo s'orriolu*
> *de dare attentu a sa tanto istimada:*
> *de cussa razza de sos traitores*
> *devo distruer manoos e minores.*

His Excellency the Prefect Gandolfo thought he was listening to a language that was no language at all. Anyone speaking

172

that language must perforce be dangerous. His moustachioed assistant, however, seemed to read the palimpsest in the parchment.

"It means," he explained, "that now he has lost all his loved ones, he can strike without fear of reprisal."

The prefect glanced at his subordinate. This crazed sergeant was beginning to get him into trouble with Rome. But the matter of law and order seemed to be under control.

"Call out the militia," he said.

The year 1926 was just a string of corpses. The drought had led to a struggle for survival, which meant killing before you were killed yourself. In 1926 anyone who had not had the foresight to lay in supplies had hunger knocking at the door.

The price on Stocchino's head had risen to 150,000 lire, higher even than the dizzying 100,000 on *su nanu Santino Succu*. Hunger leads to rashness. The Dui brothers Cosma and Damiano, who needless to say were twins, tried to lure Stocchino into a trap from which he escaped by taking shelter behind a cart. The immortal tiger did away with the twins only three weeks later. When, just before he shot them, he asked them what they had against him, their answer was that his blood money would have saved them from bankruptcy. So the death of the twins became a pageant of death. The limbs hacked off the two young men were strewn all over the village. No-one dared to pick them up. In the hand of one was a note:

In payment for the blood I have shed at your hands I sentence you to a terrible death.

> *I sign myself and remain as ever,*
> *Samuele Stocchino*

Then there was the shoemaker who hanged himself for fear of being murdered, and the Fascist militias made fools of. And the Marcialis murder that Stocchino claimed for his own but was cleared of. Sheer butchery.

But in early 1927, when Nuoro became the capital of the province, when Ottavio Dinale, the first chief of police with powers over the interior of Sardinia, installed himself in his brand-new headquarters; when Grazia Deledda became an internationally famous writer and won the Nobel Prize, but in her own country was treated like a Cassandra, then things had to change. Mussolini in person had vowed that Fascism would put an end to brigandry in Sardinia . . . So it was tit for tat: 250,000 lire for Samuele Stocchino of Arzana, dead or alive.

PART FIVE

Profound Satisfaction and Hearty Congratulations

And suddenly I find myself before a great chasm
and I see two men struggling on the ground.
Jean Giono, *Deux cavaliers de l'orage*

Stand-in

It is my desire, as Prefect and as Fascist, assuming all the responsibility of my function and my mission, out of love of your homeland, to draw forth from their cavernous lairs the maleficent forces of crime, and to destroy them. It is my desire that there should not arise any depraved legend of perverse heroism. I insist on the suppression of any kind of connivance whether active or passive, conjoined with the wretched complicity that has deformed or destroyed the most basic moral feeling. There is a heroism that must triumph, and it is our heroism, from the prefect to the carabinieri, from the militiaman to the citizen, let us go forward to the outcome . . .

Ottavio Dinale, First Prefect of Nuoro, *Announcement and Appeal to the Populace of the Province*, 10 July, 1927

I

Where we tell of a hasty departure

Saved by a miracle. Saved by a miracle, Holy Mother of God, O Blessed Virgin! Blessed be all the souls in Purgatory.

He doubled up, panting and clutching his knees. As he ran he had even managed to think up a story in case he were caught. One of those he had learned at the movies: "Now let's all take it easy, let's not judge by appearances. The honour of Donna Isabella, child-bride and countess, is unblemished. I had promised to give her fencing lessons and on my honour, I vowed to keep it secret . . ." She would then tell the same story to her ageing husband in whose mind rage would be supplanted by mere misgivings.

A woman who wanted to learn how to fence . . . Looked like a bad film, even though Conte Olivieri's mastiff-like face had never before shown any sign of suspicion.

Saverio Políto, in the flower of his virility and intemperance, had secretly visited the the bedchamber of a married lady . . . And a married lady of rank, no less than a countess: Countess Olivieri Torrepedente. The child-bride of Mussolini's "bedmat", as the count himself was secretly dubbed in the corridors of power.

As he dashed through the orange grove Saverio finished buttoning his shirt. Time had flown while in the arms of Donna Isabella, but his ears were still very alert. A moment, a bare moment later, and the count in person would have caught them in the very act.

179

Saverio Políto laughed to himself as he started on the last stretch of field there behind the oratory of Santa Brigida where the estate wall was so collapsed as to be "just an open gate", as Donna Isabella had let slip as if by mistake. Once past that, under cover and trusting in some farmhands who would keep their mouths shut as only the chink of money could make them, he would reach his car.

When he reached the door of the farmhouse he knocked three times, then twice and finally a single hefty rap. The woman inside ran to open it for him with lowered head.

"Wine!" commanded Saverio, laying his hat on a box seat. The woman hurried to fetch the jug.

"I wasn't expecting you so soon, Your Excellency," apologised the woman. "Tiberio has just gone to get the car ready."

Saverio held out his glass for more wine. Tiberio hurried in through a back door, sweating, cap in hand.

"Everything's ready, Your Excellency," he murmured deferentially.

"Good," said Saverio, picking up his hat. As he started to pull on his gloves he contrived to let a few coins fall on the table.

The woman scooped them up at once, as if they would have gone down in value had they lain too long on her table.

"Always at your service, Your Excellency, always at your service," she said as she noticed the emolument had been more than expected, more than the last time.

But Saverio had no time for thanks or good wishes – he could not find his left glove. Anxiously he scrutinised the rough stone floor of the room. The glove was not there. The man and the woman watched him without daring to ask what was up.

"My glove!" he blurted out, in a voice that seemed to have lost all the self-confidence of just a moment before. "I've got to go back . . ." he went on, muttering to himself.

Eyes glued to the ground, he hurried back along the route he had taken to reach the farmhouse. He reached the gap in the wall of Count Olivieri's country estate, opposite the semi-circular apse of the little oratory of Santa Brigida. He crossed the orange grove till he came to the conservatory of the villa itself. He climbed the ivy-covered pergola right up to his lover's balcony . . .

The next morning Ninetta entered his bedroom. Touching his shoulder lightly she awakened him.

"Your father," she whispered.

Saverio opened his eyes. "What's the time?" he asked in surprise.

"It's late. Your father has called for you and wants to see you at once," she said, opening the curtains to let in the daylight.

"Just time enough to get ready," said Saverio, sitting up on the side of the bed.

The old woman kissed the crucifix hanging round her neck. "Today is not a good day," she said with a sob. "There's such confusion." She then disappeared into the next room, to reappear a few minutes later with a basin of steaming water and some clean cloths over her forearm.

Saverio in the meantime had stood up, completely naked.

Ninetta placed the basin on the floor and soaked one of the cloths. With swift, gentle movements she ran over his legs with the wet cloth, rising to her feet to reach his armpits, his neck, his face, then moved round him to wash his calves, his buttocks, his back.

Saverio stood there with his eyes still half closed, enjoying the damp warmth on his body.

The woman went on with her work in a crescendo of eagerness. "You're beautiful, my angel, you're so beautiful," she murmured from time to time. "You're my beautiful child . . ."

Saverio arched his neck and closed his eyes, and seizing her hand guided it firmly to his lower parts.

"Here you are at last!" burst out General Augusto Políto.

"Couldn't get ready any quicker," apologised Saverio. "Were you wanting to speak to me?"

The general irritably gestured to him to take a seat.

"Why d'you think I sent for you? I have something to tell you and you won't like it. In a week's time you'll be off to Sardinia!"

"A week? Sardinia?" echoed Saverio.

"You've got it! I've obtained a post for you from Count Olivieri. You've been appointed Il Duce's special commissioner for security in Barbagia. They need youngsters of rank in those parts. Il Duce in person has expressed his approval and you'll be taking orders directly from Rome."

"But just like this . . . without warning . . ."

"It's a very tricky job . . . The situation is such . . . You will arrive in Barbagia incognito."

Saverio struggled to keep his calm. "What situation are you talking about?"

General Políto heaved a heavy sigh. He stood up and went to the window.

"You are my son and I won't beat about the bush. The truce arranged some time ago with the local brigands in Barbagia has been broken, our agreement with the bandits there, which I have always opposed, has not had the results we hoped for," he said after a pause and without looking round.

This provoked no visible reaction in Saverio: "So what?"

"It is that Il Duce has gone to personal lengths to assert that Sardinia is wholly and in every way a reclaimed territory. But there's a problem, and a big one . . ."

Saverio Políto compressed his lips and made a haughty gesture.

"And what has that got to do with me, may I ask?" he demanded.

"You know him."

Saverio stared at his father. "Sergeant Samuele Stocchino," spelled out the general.

Saverio at once succeeded in putting a face to that name. "An animal," he said.

"Your task will be to rout that animal out," said the general with perfect sangfroid. "You will have absolute freedom of action."

"If that's the way it is, I'll go. May I retire now?"

"One more thing, a piece of advice. Live a secluded life this coming week, because the less you're seen around the better!"

"Am I under house arrest?"

The general shook his head, but could not suppress a laugh.

"It's a piece of good advice from Count Olivieri, with which I heartily concur . . ."

II

*In which we tell of a gloomy arrival . . . and
certain local plottings*

To Saverio Políto, Sardinia looked like a motionless black whale smothered in seaweed, the muddy shell of a monstrous turtle, a blacker black than the black water. For sixteen hours the ship had glided across a greenish, gelatinous sea, and now there it was: the island.

Since the war he had suffered from claustrophobia, and that slow crossing seemed to be taking him nowhere. So he spent most of those sixteen hours on deck watching the efforts of the prow to force its way through that solid-seeming sea.

He had never known such a mournful winter, even when at the front, or ever seen such a weird light.

The bright moon, low on the horizon, printed the shadow of his nose, a dark wedge, from his cheekbone to his ill-shaven chin. And he liked it. That nose, and that chin, were his best features, because his eyes, for example, were small and too close together, withdrawn into deep sockets kept in perpetual darkness by the rocky ledges of his brows. His mouth, a good inch and a half beneath his nostrils when closed, might have been a horizontal pencil mark.

He might have been navigating some watercourse in Amazonia, such as had been described to him by those fearless souls who had penetrated such uncharted places, air green with foliage that rose so high as to screen off the sky. It is hard to draw breath there, because in that freshwater sea, as in this salt one, there is no air. His heart beat so hard that it thumped in his ears. He had sometimes felt this way as a child.

The port stank horribly. The stench of death and livestock and diesel oil and coal. If the sea had never seemed so hostile to Saverio Políto, the land appeared no better. Throughout his journey into the interior the sun determined to stay concealed. But the sky was not grey and overcast. It was greenish, somewhat like the colour of fresh-pressed olive oil, with a few yellowish streaks. No clouds to be seen. In the unbroken, stifling air of that sky even the birds were stilled. Not a breath of wind on the island: everything seemed engulfed by a membranous web.

For his transport in Barbagia they had allocated him a small truck with a local driver, Antonello Cappai da Buddusò, who had learned to drive on the Carso front.

Antonello Cappai da Buddusò was living proof of how questionable is the stereotype of the taciturn Sardinian. This one metre fifty-three centimetres of driver, the same height as His Majesty the King, to give you an idea, began to talk before even getting into the truck. All he had been told was that he was to take a mainland representative to Arzana, and this seemed to him rather odd: what on earth had a mainland representative to do in Arzana? And representative of what, might he ask? And from what part of the mainland, might he ask? He had been on the mainland when called up in 1897. And instead of going to the front he very nearly ended up at Avezzano, did Políto know Avezzano? Terrible earthquake there, really terrible . . . To cut a long story short, he was about to be sent to Avezzano to help the earthquake victims when at the last moment up came this lieutenant and asked if anyone was interested in going into the "motor corps". Well, Antonello Cappai da Buddusò didn't have the foggiest as to who these might be. They sounded like walking corpses to him, but up went his hand, 'cause that's the way he is: act first and think later. So they selected him and transferred him from the troops to be sent to Avezzano to help the earthquake victims to that of the motor corps in Vicenza. He had been at Monte Berico, or to be more exact at Villa Clementi, know that? And they had put him into advanced drivers' school, to become a driver for the high command, where they told him he was made for the job, and only two months later he was tearing up and down the Veneto driving General Pecori Girali. And this was really funny, because when you came down to it who could a Sardinian driver drive if not *Pecori* . . . ?* And ha, ha, bursts of laughter, got it? You understand? Have you ever been to war?

Políto had kept his eyes shut, but as the truck was rattling around even more than ever, he opened them again. He asked where they were, now that the truck had started up a gentle slope.

"Mont'Albo," came the reply. Then, waving at the sea, the chatterbox of a driver uttered mysterious words: *Sa preda bianca, Contone malu, Isteria* . . . And then, as they climbed into the mountains: *Marreri, Sa e Sulis . . . e Mamoiada* . . . And so on and so forth. They were going to a really lovely spot, the Ogliastra, he said, but did he know that in that area there was a ferocious bandit? Samuele Stocchino! The very name strikes terror in you. D'you know it? But what a silly question, idiot that I am . . . What can those people over on the mainland possibly know about a backwater like this? But it's not a bit true, what they say about Stocchino killing just for the fun of it, that he simply kills at random. He's followed the same path, step by step, for years now, and never a problem. Stocchino knows who he's got it in for, all too well.

*

* *"Pecore"* means "sheep", at that time the main livelihood of much of Sardinia.

By now the sky had become a greenish-grey sheet above their heads. Políto felt hot, hot enough to sweat, but it wasn't really hot. It was just that words and breath had positively saturated the truck's cab. Or maybe it was only the uphill hairpin bends that Cappai took with a flourish, without much caution. And meanwhile he talked . . . Do you know what that lunatic Stocchino pulled off one time? He got a job as a pieceworker dressed up as a woman, believe it or not. With a headscarf and skirt and his face as smooth as a young girl's . . . They say that in those clothes no-one would have realised he was a man, least of all a sergeant with medals to his name, and not one of those men who think they're really women, eh? – if you see what I mean. In any case, when word spread that he was looking for day labour, for fear of reprisals all the land-owners immediately took on viragos to work for them, *màscrine* as they're called here. Or take that time he was caught dressed as a gypsy and sent on his way by a police sergeant with a kick up the arse, well, that evening when he got home the sergeant found tucked into his pistol holster a message of only two words: "Samuele Stocchino" . . . Not to mention the time he dressed as a nun to meet his fiancée in church, or when he heard his sworn enemy's confession instead of the priest . . . "Oh, yes, this Stocchino is quite a joker, *brulleri*, as we say . . ."

Now Saverio understood the word *brulleri*, but he under-stood it in his own way. He saw before him the melancholy face of Corporal Stocchino as he was about to strike: that almost serene, almost encouraging expression had all the markings of an unholy joy. A joker indeed was Samuele Stocchino, with two wars behind him. Ah yes, you could say that again.

Still, by the grace of God they reached Arzana. Which might not be the centre of the world, but at least had some semblance of civilisation. It seemed incredible that, in remote times, a group of human beings had actually decided to settle in the midst of all that rugged wilderness. There is no river here, so to find cultivable land one has to go down into the valley or scrape away at the living rock. The sea is close by, but the air is not sea air. So Saverio Políto drew in as much as he could of it as he stretched his legs.

But already Private Cappai was asking him if he had arranged for somewhere to stay, and said that some distant cousins of his knew a woman who had rooms to let, a widow, with a big house, very clean and tidy . . .

III

*In which we speak of Nuoro as capital
of the province and what bigmouths
the Nuorese are . . . and tell another tale
about boots*

Yo la quería con toda el alma.

"Without ever raising your feet from the floor! Look, Sergeant-Major, you're lifting them!"

Es tan grande el dolor, que no puedo llorar!

"Slow there, and don't look down at your feet."

"Ah, to hell with it."

Donde estás corazón, non oigo el tu palpitar . . . ?

Sergeant-Major Palmas freed himself from the embrace of Lance-Corporal Butto. Hipólito Lázaro continued to sing as if blowing into a penny whistle. Palmas, when all is said, had never even liked Lázaro: he was a Caruso buff. That fount of pure water. Butto gave him a look.

"I don't care for this Lázaro one bit," said the sergeant.

"You need to persist," said Butto.

"Perhaps with a beautiful woman, mind . . ." said his superior with a shake of the head.

Butto puckered his lips. "With all due respect," he said, "if there were a beautiful woman . . . there'd have been no need to learn the tango, would there? And then, you're not following properly: one, two, three, four . . ." And he went on dancing on his own.

In the corridor of the ex-monastery, now the carabinieri

barracks of Arzana, Lázaro's voice sounded like that of a corpse come back to life.

La quería yo tanto y se fué para no retornar.

But everything – the rasp of the dance steps, the bleating voice of the old tenor, the sergeant's baritone – every darned thing boomed and re-echoed as it rose towards the pretentious cross-vaulted ceiling. Pretentious and shoddy plasterwork, because the intention was good, but there had been no time for finesse in the old monastery, now a barracks.

So, pressed close, belly to belly, the sergeant and the lance-corporal moved in time to the music.

"We don't have any information, at least not officially," said Butto, harking back to an earlier conversation.

"About the mainlander who's living at widow Cocco's?"

"In the corn trade," replied the corporal. "But you're losing the rhythm, sergeant. You were doing so well . . ."

The tango rebounded off the dazzling whiteness of the walls. On Palmas this tango had the effect of a woman one should be wary of, but he persisted all the same, trying to keep the time set by Butto.

"If they send a special commissioner from Rome I ought to be informed," muttered the sergeant.

The corporal waited until he had finished his pirouette before saying, "They might not tell us, but they'll certainly let them know at Nuoro."

"What's that?" cried the sergeant, disconcerted and losing his rhythm. "Just because they've become provincial capital on account of that strumpet Grazia Deledda, do they imagine Rome would keep them in the know?"

The corporal burst out laughing. "I wouldn't say strumpet, sergeant. D'you realise what sort of prize she's won?" The sergeant had no intention of being sidetracked and went on dancing despite the fact that the record had ended a while ago.

"You're doing well," the corporal added encouragingly. It almost seemed that the absence of music had aided the sergeant's concentration.

"No, I don't know what prize it is," said the latter suddenly. "What is it?" he insisted, seeing that the other did not answer.

"Big stuff," replied Butto. "They say they're talking about it all over the world."

"So that means that we're not in this world," said the sergeant, "because I've never heard of it."

"What do you expect them to tell us, Sergeant, now that they're listening to those bigmouths in Nuoro, as if their mouths weren't big enough before . . . ? If they've sent a special commissioner from Rome, they'll have had their own reasons for doing so, after what happened in Seui last April . . ."

The story goes that Stocchino needed a new pair of boots. But he could not set foot in town because he had refused to make a pact with the local Fascist bosses. Other fugitives had reached agreements and were allowed to come back and sleep with their wives, outlaws though they were.

What they had not understood about the "tiger" was that he was waging a war against himself. You could not tell Samuele that a peace pact with the government was a good thing all round. For him, the only conceivable good thing was to assuage the fury within him. But that could not be explained. Therefore, without even knowing how, he had become "enemy number one". Or rather, exactly "how" this had happened was plain enough. It was because the people he threatened hid themselves in their black shirts, because beneath the black shirt you could hide almost anything, just like sweeping it under the carpet.

As far as Rome was concerned, Stocchino mattered as much or as little as the Nobel Prize for Literature won by Grazia Deledda did to Sergeant Palmas: less than nothing. But he began to matter only when he became a symbol. Manai, Bardi and the rest of them may have been in hiding in their houses, but they had powerful friends in Nuoro, who had powerful friends in Cagliari, who had powerful friends in Rome. So when a name was mentioned, when it was spoken out loud, that meant it had begun to exist. And if that name was pronounced in the very office of Benito Mussolini, and what's more in the presence of Mussolini himself, that meant that it had passed from being nothing to being everything. A sergeant, too, and even worse, a Great War hero decorated for gallantry!

It so happened that Stocchino knew a cobbler in Seui whom he could trust. In his usual manner, he woke him in the dead of night and the cobbler got up at once to draw a pattern and take measurements. His feet were very slender and white, and fearsomely clean. And cold. Before disturbing the cobbler he had gone to the village pump to wash them and put on clean socks. The cobbler heard him cough while he was handling those tiny feet, almost waxen, like those of a dying man. Seen in the light of a single candle he looked like a youngster, with that wispy beard that just refused to grow any longer. His eyes had the fixed, intense look of sadness of a man trying to choke back tears. His eyes were red-ringed as if perpetually feverish. So the measurements were taken and the boots would be ready in a week. Stocchino asked how much it would come to and the cobbler said, "Oh, nothing."

"There's no such thing as nothing," said Stocchino. "Give me your price for the boots."

The cobbler looked at his feet and said they could talk about that next week . . . In the meantime he gave him a piece of leather to slip inside his worn-out boot to keep out the wet, at least for the week.

But Samuele did not like that refusal of money at all, any more than the fact that the cobbler had kept his eyes on the ground the whole time. That was not fear, because Samuele could detect the smell of fear on anyone. No, what the cobbler showed was not fear but shame. So Samuele, prey to doubt, stopped just a short way from the cobbler's house and after about five minutes saw him come out. In the dead silence of the night he made his way to the tavern. For Stocchino anything was sufficient to make him unrecognisable, so he lifted a sheep-skin coat from a cart standing nearby, pulled the hood over his head and went into the tavern. By now he was standing right behind the cobbler, who was deep in conversation with a black-shirted young man. Samuele, who could hear what they said, pretended not to hear because such things were hurtful to him. So he left the tavern weighed down by a terrible sadness. He had with him a little blouse of Mariangela's, so he raised it to his nose so as to feel her deep in his lungs.

A week later no-one came to fetch the boots. Two cara-binieri and two Blackshirt militiamen were posted at the four corners of the courtyard of the cobbler's house. They heard a noise, cocked their rifles and stood at the ready, but it was only a small boy. The boy entered the shop and without a word handed the cobbler a message. He then asked for a couple of pennies as he had been told to by the man who had asked him to run the errand. When the boy went away, the cobbler was left alone holding the message, staring at it without unfolding it. He knew only too well that it was his death warrant, and he began to wail. The cobbler's wails grew more and more horrifying, and the carabinieri and Blackshirts outside realised something was going on. But they had a moment of hesitation because it was truly impossible that anyone apart from the boy could have passed unobserved. By the time the four of them met in the middle of the courtyard the cobbler's wails had ceased. So they rushed into the shop and found him hanging, his legs still jerking like those of a puppet. The note on the floor beneath him, written in a pointed script, bore the words: *Will you do it or shall I?*

"Anyway, I'll tell you what the special commissioner is here for," said Sergeant Palmas, wrapped in thought. Corporal Butto pulled away from him as if their positions in the dancing lesson made anything confidential all the more scandalous.

"What is he here for?" he asked after a time, seeing that the sergeant could not make up his mind to continue.

"To take the blood money back to Rome. First they strike a bargain and then they regret it . . ."

"The fact is, Sergeant, with all due respect, they can put any price they like on Stocchino's head, but no-one has the guts to inform on him."

The sergeant agreed. How could he deny the fact after ten years?

Indeed, for ten long years Samuele Stocchino had managed to elude all attempts to capture him. And not even an enormous price on his head, the biggest ever offered for a bandit, had been of any use. The legend of his immortality had become an absolute certainty. At least three times he had been presumed dead, but he had always reappeared. Always. The local land-owners had tried everything, but the result was that some of them had been forced to sell up, while others imprisoned themselves in their own houses.

Hence the unexpected arrival of the corn merchant did not go unnoticed.

The lad walked two or three paces ahead of him. With confident strides he set off down the street across Bainzu Pais's courtyard. He plunged into a maze of alleyways leading to the parish church of San Giovanni Battista. Saverio Políto followed him in silence. It would have been senseless to ask for information from a servant of the Manai family. The youngster looked back several times to make sure the mainlander was still there behind him. In his message, Prefect Dinale had insisted that they go on foot. The meeting had to be kept secret and he could not risk anyone seeing the hoofmarks of Políto's horse anywhere near the Oratorio dei Nobili. So he had acted accordingly.

When they came to the church the boy pointed to an alley to the right of the steps. "They're waiting for you," he said in a timid little voice before going off in the opposite direction to the one he had indicated.

The main door of the oratory stood ajar. Inside there was just enough light to prevent him from stumbling. Saverio Políto took a few steps forward along the narrow nave. He smelled the aggressive stench of candles and incense, and heard behind him the sharp snap of the door shutting. He turned instinctively to see who had come in after him and discerned a portly, clerical figure, although before he could see him he heard his wheezing breath.

"You have arrived," panted old Father Marci as he came to meet him, and laying a flabby hand on his shoulder he escorted him towards a small side altar.

The prefect, Ottavio Dinale, was wrapped in a heavy cloak. Now that Políto's eyes had become accustomed to the darkness he could make out two other figures beyond him. The first was that of an old man whose white hair shone in the candlelight. The second was a fat man whose face was half hidden by a stocking cap.

The prefect invited him to take a seat.

"Forgive us for summoning you without warning, and to such an unusual place," he began, "but it is absolutely essential that this meeting should remain secret." Saverio Políto shook his head as if to say that he needed no such preamble. The prefect received the gesture with a smile. "Don Giacomo Manai," he said, indicating the old man. Saverio Políto gave him a slight nod. The old man replied with a movement of his hands that had all the brusque impatience of someone accustomed to giving orders. "Don Giovanni Bardi," the prefect continued. "They wished to meet you," he added with such warmth as one might use when speaking to a child.

"And to make you a proposition," the old man cut in. Above his head was an altarpiece of fine workmanship. A Virgin of the Rosary emerged from it in a mire of colour dimmed by the smoke from the candles. Even the face of the Madonna had taken on the same waxy, yellowish tinge. Don Giacomo Manai's white beard wagged up and down as he spoke. "We have decided to put to you some extremely delicate questions," he said, pausing to search for the appropriate words.

Don Giovanni Bardi nodded deferentially. He was much the younger of the two, and his bulk – he must have weighed nearly a hundred kilos – caused him to sweat copiously beneath his traditional Sardinian costume.

"We are speaking of your mission," Prefect Dinale concluded, at a loss for a more tactful way of putting it. Saverio Políto turned to meet his gaze. "We live on the fringes of the empire, but even we have our informants in the capital," the prefect continued, stressing this last word to give it due importance.

"Then you know more about it than I do," Políto replied, unperturbed.

"Yes, yes," the prefect said sceptically. "But without wishing to give offence, we are not completely behind the times."

"You must realise how much trust and honour . . ." Don Giovanni Bardi put in, taking advantage of the prefect's pause for reflection.

"Young man, have you got the idea?" broke in Don Giacomo

Manai. "We are talking about that monster Samuele Stocchino."

"Gentlemen . . ." Saverio Políto said, rising to his feet.

Prefect Dinale gave him a stare.

"Easy now, easy. Please listen." Saverio Políto sat down again. "We know who you are, where you come from and who sent you," he stated with emphasis. Don Giovanni Bardi nodded his great head in agreement.

"Then you know more than I do," repeated Políto. "And now, if you will allow me . . . if you will *all* allow me . . ." And he started to get to his feet again.

"We know where he is," Giacomo Manai said.

"Go and get him then."

Prefect Dinale gave a sniff: "The idea was . . ."

"You know him well," Giovanni Bardi said.

"I am a corn merchant," rebutted Políto.

"Of course, of course," agreed the prefect. "Let us say that this novel occupation does not prevent us from helping each other."

"A lot of people in our town would thank you for ridding us of him," Father Marci said.

"Only in our town?" Bardi queried.

"They'll put up a statue to you even in Nuoro," Don Giacomo Manai declared, laying it on thick. "You will have observed that fate has endowed me with a determined old age. Do you know how old I am?" Políto shook his head. "Ninety," said the old man. "I am ninety years old because these eyes of mine cannot close forever until they see Samuele Stocchino dead and buried."

"What are you asking of me?" demanded Políto at that point.

Dinale hesitated a moment or two before replying. The air inside the oratory had become heavy with grease from the candles and the whole flickering scene was like a dream. Bardi

197

adjusted his stocking cap, pulling it even further down over his forehead.

"You undoubtedly have something that we don't have," the prefect asserted. Políto waited for him to go on. And so he did: "You have had means of knowing Stocchino in person and we have reason to think that he trusts you . . ."

"A bait," concluded Manai. "Name your price and you will get it."

"A worm on a hook," said Políto as if to himself. "Wriggling in front of the fish." A terrible silence fell over the little chapel, and the tiny vault sent back exactly the same: silence.

Silence.

Políto took stock of his interlocutors. Manai was wearing the black shirt, as was Dinale. On his traditional costume Bardi sported the badge of the Fascist regime. After a long pause Políto said, "You gave assurances. In Rome they are not satisfied with your results."

Everyone present became aware that his tone of voice had changed. Everyone realised that the moment had come to drop the mask.

Dinale leaned forward: "Your Excellency," he said, "you can see for yourself that it's harder than one might think. It is not the will that is lacking, but the orders from Rome were scarcely exhaustive."

Bardi was about to speak, but Políto silenced him with a glare.

"The orders were appropriate. I would not like to have to report to Rome that they have been questioned by those instructed to carry them out." Dinale stared, open-eyed, as if total darkness had fallen in the room. "You are not up against an ordinary man," Políto pointed out, addressing Manai. "The way you hate each other doesn't keep only you going, but him as well."

"It's all very well for you to talk. But I can't even leave my house and neither can my relations. My livestock is not looked after, my land is covered in weeds and two of my sons have been killed." For the first time Giacomo Manai's voice betrayed his age.

"We are obviously wasting our time," said Bardi, getting to his feet with some effort.

"I would prefer a private talk with you," Políto told Dinale. Dinale looked from face to face. "Any problems?" asked Políto. Bardi closed his eyes. Manai shook his head. Dinale gestured to Father Marci to move aside out of the oratory doorway and the priest did so.

"I don't care who you have to answer to, *cavaliere*, but I know who I have to answer to," Políto said, once they were alone.

"I understand your position, but Rome has to understand that without the support of the local landowners . . ."

"I will give you Stocchino, but the price on his head stays in Rome."

Dinale's face froze in an inscrutable expression.

"I know that you would have sought an agreement if Stocchino had permitted it." Dinale rode that blow and started to answer it. But a look from Políto stopped him. "The reputation of the Government and the interests of the Party take precedence, *cavaliere*."

"Very good. Let it be done for the good of the Motherland, the interests of the Party and the reputation of the Government in our province."

"I see that we've understood each other. You will be informed of where and how. And tell your friends that they have nothing to gain from all this. Nothing at all, you understand?"

Políto got up to leave, but Dinale stopped him: "How do you intend to move?"

"Simply to move, that's all," said Políto. "To listen, to let myself be seen and to sell seeds. That's what I'm here for. I don't have to go looking for anyone, but whoever wants me will find me. Of that you may be sure."

IV

The hunter

Every morning in that land of exile, in his austere little room in widow Cocco's boarding house, he had peered into a stained mirror precariously supported by the flimsy iron framework of the washstand and had seen his face, which was that of the empire to come. And giving himself affectionate little pats to prepare the rough skin for the razor's edge, he told himself that those jaws, those very jaws, were his strong point, that they induced respect in those uncouth Barbagians and village troglodytes. But more than anything they aroused bad feelings in the local women, with their rumps like mares'; they had always been distrustful of handsome men. Smiling behind their kerchiefs, they looked for other qualities: character, manliness and (though they would not admit it) a touch of arrogance, which they called *barrosìa*. And *barra*, in fact, in their incomprehensible language, was the word for "jaw". One like that of Il Duce himself, whom the good Lord had unquestionably endowed with good looks, those of some stony deity, of a warm-blooded, complex he-man with full, pouting lips, a generous, prolific father, a stallion good for battle or for breeding, a gentleman, workman and peasant, and a warlord to boot. With all this flitting through his mind, he felt an awakening between his thighs . . .

Every morning, then, before the mirror on widow Cocco's washstand, Saverio Polìto, the great man of law, the very man whom Mussolini himself had put in charge of the Barbagia, while venerating his sacred matutinal erection, mowed the black stubble from his face and thought about his enemy. But in both cases it was a labour of Sisyphus, for his beard darkened his chin again only a few hours after being eradicated, while his enemy, Samuele Stocchino, the outlawed beast of Arzana, no sooner seemed to be caught than he vanished into thin air. And three, four, even five overpaid informers spotted him at one and the same time at Ingurtosu and at Strisaili, at Santa Barbara and at Baunei, or else told him he was helping that madman Meloni to raise ostriches, cleaning ancient roundhouses at Monte Spada, praying in church and fornicating in a brothel in Cagliari. For Samuele Stocchino, ferocious and unruffled, was everywhere yet nowhere.

To rout out the beast you had to become one yourself. But Saverio Polìto, as they whispered at the Ministry of the Interior, had always had something of the beast in him – ever since the time of that orgy at Fiume, when the poet D'Annunzio had put him at the head of a pagan procession wearing the horns of a faun and playing pan pipes.

To match up to Samuele Stocchino, the tiger of Ogliastra who caused Il Duce sleepless nights, he had therefore had to return to the primitive state, become the primordial Fascist. On his mission in the crucible of humanity he had been forced to display his most base inclinations. For this reason, even in winter, he went around with his black shirt open to reveal the mat of black hair on his chest.

Before the yawning mouth of the fireplace, widow Cocco was roasting chestnuts. Saverio Polìto stood eyeing her hips and buttocks for a moment or two before making his presence known. Then he murmured a good evening. The woman spun round and looked at him as if she had seen a ghost, so scared that she crossed herself. She said she had not heard him come in. Then her eyes moved to his open shirt and she asked him if he was not cold. Saverio Políto replied that no, he did not feel the cold. Then she happened to mention the fact that she had been cursed with a lonely life when still in the bloom of youth. And she heard him speak of his own loneliness. Shortly afterwards, on the bed in that austere little room, he allowed himself to be taken, though with all the confident self-control of a grown-up man feigning resistance, while she ate him up with the desperation of a drowning woman. Famished, unable to control her movements, serving only her need, she had forced his hands to clasp her ample breasts and he allowed himself to be led, with a foretaste of the pleasurable time to come, when the first frenzy is over and gives place to a slow rhythm, and the famished lover to the gourmet. And so he continued to pleasure her until she fell prostrate on top of him. And in that prostration her body sang. Indeed widow Cocco could not believe her body as it relished a neverending sequel, and she begged him to stop, then to go on, and to go on over and over. Her face pressed to his hairy chest, she breathed the aroma of lime and citronella. Because now he was on top of her, slow and relentless, his gaze drowned in the depths of her face, his mouth pouting as in a soundless whistle, that gnarled body as of a barbarous Christ, rigid where she was yielding . . . He knew when to recognise the moment, and knew that she would too . . . And indeed, when the moment came, she clutched his loins, sinking her nails into his flesh and crying out to the rhythm of his thrusts . . .

Afterwards they ate the chestnuts. She talked away to cover her shame. But it was more triumph than shame, because she had been hoping for it ever since Políto had set foot in her house. There's no denying it, the body thinks for itself. It thinks with the nose, with the eyes, and then with the hands. And then with all the rest . . .

She told the story of the sign on the ground in front of the house, the sign made by Felice Stocchino's boot when the cooper refused him a drink of water. A letter "S" which they tried in vain to get rid of. In vain because it seemed to have grooved itself into the very subsoil. So much so that the old woman of the house, Gesuina Lindiri, the cooper's mother, by constantly pestering her son to do something about it, forced him to dig a hole where the letter was and plant a laurel bush there. But it was no good. The plant died, as did all the others they went on planting. Thus it was that the terrible power of the sign was clearly seen; for when the last bush had withered and the wind had levelled the ground, there was the letter "S", traced by the foot of the offended wayfarer, exactly as it had been before, even clearer than before. At which Gesuina Lindiri pointed a finger to the heavens and rushed off to pay for a novena to Our Lady of Mercy. Then she implored her son to go to Felice Stocchino and make amends, giving him salt and coffee and sugar for the family, since he had so many mouths to feed . . .

She, widow Cocco, spoke of these things in an attempt to draw Saverio Políto out of the silence in which he had wrapped himself. She spoke of the killing, the widow, without any reason for doing so. Políto watched her with tight lips, as if trying to guide her narrative with his eyes alone. And in fact she ended by telling him about the night of Saint Sebastian's day. Yes indeed, that business with the cooper had been really and truly terrible: the whole family exterminated.

Every one of them dead . . .

V

In which we narrate the absurd way it all began

The mountain winter was a torment of stabbing pinpricks, a sheet of ice pressed to one's back, the glare of marble in a morgue. He had decided to travel by night, in the biting cold, because in those parts a man who goes about alone at night is regarded with respect. He left the small huddle of houses that was the village and plunged into the rustling, grunting and crackling of the open country. He had ventured out along the old nuraghic sheep track so as to avoid the mail-coach road, the new public highway that took a shorter route. Low on the horizon the moon, full of itself, cast the darkest of shadows on his face. But Saverio Políto did not really care, for from where he was staying at widow Cocco's house it was not far to the house of the killing.

Accompanied by the sickening stench of terebinth trees, heralded by the clatter of horseshoes on granite flagstones, he caught sight of the place. It was a low farmhouse building surrounded by a dry-stone wall. Without dismounting he passed the delapidated gate that had once marked the entrance to the property. Then, blowing on his bunched fists to warm them, he looked around him. A scrawny stray dog came towards him from behind the house. The high commissioner dismounted to stroke his tousled coat and reached into his saddlebag for a scrap of bread and cheese rind. The dog inspected him for a moment before gobbling down the unexpected gift, but Saverio Políto was already lighting the acetylene lamp that had been part of his equipment in the army special services. An unhinged wooden door leaned up against the wall beside the gaping black mouth of the entrance to the building. Step by step the cone of light from the lamp penetrated the squalor of the cooper's house, abandoned to its destiny. In graveyard solitude, as widow Cocco had put it, hurriedly crossing herself. Because too many had met their deaths in that house and all were roving through those rooms, seeking the reason for that butchery on the night of Saint Sebastian. Not even the cooper's own relations had had any wish to take possession of those walls, nor even of the land, leaving it to the crows and the wind, and good luck to them. So over the years it had been occupied by pigs, given shelter to the occasional wayfarer, and had been a place for children to play in . . .

Saverio Políto attempted to get his bearings. He made out the stairwell rising two yards from the entrance and felt the cracked flooring beneath his heavy boots. He shone his lamp on a part of the staircase wall, marked with a long, rust-red stain. It must have been the blood of the cooper's eldest daughter, killed while trying to escape. At least, that's what they said . . . Which in cases like this, in this accursed hole, was as good as saying nothing.

The story of this blood, for instance . . .

It was then that he heard a sound, but he could not be sure if it was a sign of danger. One thing one learns in war is that there are dangerous sounds and harmless ones. What Políto heard at that moment was the faint sound of breathing. He turned his light towards it. In a corner of the room which some shepherd had used as a doss-down he saw a heap of rags, and protruding from it two boots and two legs clad in khaki puttees.

"Lieutenant . . ." came a whisper.

"Corporal Stocchino," Políto said, pointing the beam of his lamp towards the voice.

By its light Stocchino's face seemed as if imprinted on a white sheet. His eyes had a spectral look, his mouth was a slash, like a scar between his nose and his chin. It was not hard to understand what feverish tenacity kept him alive.

"Sergeant," he murmured. "They made me a sergeant." Políto gave a nod. "Have they sent you to look for me, Lieutenant?" Stocchino enquired from the depths of the room.

Políto nodded again. "You've had us worried," he said.

"I am dying," the other replied simply. "I won't last long, Lieutenant."

Políto noticed that Stocchino was shivering, so he cast an eye around. In the wall was the skeleton of a fireplace. He searched for some dry sticks with which to light a fire. In the flame-lit room Stocchino's face took on a touch of colour.

At a certain point he cried, "Don't you hear them?" Políto pricked up his ears. He heard nothing. He shook his head.

"It's full of voices in here . . . Full of voices . . . That's why I come here . . ."

The night of the killing. The full moon was drinking from a horizon as jagged as the edge of an eggshell broken in two, indolent almost as death itself, as though in its first sleep.

The cooper's house eighteen years later. There was a point to it, Samuele told himself, since it was in the origin of things that the end may be found. And so it happened: in desperation madness lurks. January 20, 1920. Saint Sebastian, martyred with arrows.

Who knows for how long he had roved around the silent house? But we may well understand the desperation with which Samuele sought to give a name to what he thought it was his duty to do. He had struggled with himself as only he knew how, without bothering with self-deception, but needling himself, telling himself that he was a coward to strike his enemy in his sleep. Then he saw the "S" on the ground. Can such things happen? Can it be that a mark made with the toe of a boot remains fixed for twenty years in friable soil? Nonetheless, that mark made him understand once and for all the reason for his circling that house. The silence was unnatural. Even the dogs, scenting a beast, were cowering in their kennels. Samuele leaped over the low boundary wall and reached the back of the house.

The door leading into the vegetable garden gave way easily and without a sound. Once in the house he was greeted by a cat which rubbed itself in silence against his legs, and by the acrid smell of a doused fire coming from the kitchen. This he entered, with shafts of moonlight illuminating the plain, tidy room. On the marble-topped table stood a jug of water and a glass. Samuele poured himself a glassful and drained it in a draught. So the girl appeared down the stairs as if out of nowhere. And she must have thought she was seeing a ghost, because she did not even have time to shriek or cry for help. The knife cut off any reaction she might have planned. All she saw was a soldier, a young man in uniform – but there is no point in describing what she did not have time to articulate.

Pasquina Boi, the youngest daughter of Emerenziano the cooper, perished thus, without a sound, at fourteen years of age. She slipped to the ground in total silence. To reach the stairs and the upper floor Samuele had to step over her body. No tale can tell the determination with which he offered himself to the horror that was himself. He knew that the voice screaming within him was the voice of his enemy, and he also knew that it would not cease to scream with the death of the cooper or any substitute, because lives do not end with death. He climbed the stairs with all his own dead upon his shoulders. Every step was a step towards the end. Felice dead on the kitchen chair. Gonario dead through the folly of pure chance. And grandmother Basilia simply dead and gone. And Ignazia . . . Woe, alas, they would never come back.

So, without a sound, he opened the first door in the passage and leaped to the bed: Giuseppe Boi, the cooper's thirty-year-old third son, and his wife, Barbara Patteri, twenty-seven, slid straight from sleep into death, and they were the lucky ones. That made three. The second door squeaked a little. The room was used as a larder, and smelled of sausages and cheese, dried broad beans and figs. There was no-one sleeping amidst all this plenty. Felice and Gonario whispered to him to stop, urged him to take this bounty as a token that there might be such a thing as Paradise, but he chose to pay no heed to their pleas, for he saw that abundance as an expression of all that had been wrested from him. The shade of Basilia chided her grandson for not heeding even those who had loved him. But at that moment Samuele did not remember ever having been loved. He entered the room which had been that of Gesuina Lindiri, widow Boi and matriarch of the family. There he saw what he could not possibly have seen: the very last moments of the old woman on her deathbed, still urging them to get rid of the letter "S" which Felice Stocchino had traced on the ground in front of the house. But now on the bed there was a sleeping girl. The full moon lit up her form. Samuele looked at the sleeper and this was a mistake, for he knew that looking at her would would mean facing up to the horror he was committing. Indeed this came home to him when Luigia Marianna Boi, the cooper's elder daughter, opened her eyes. She thought that what she saw was no more than the incarnation of the nightmare she had grown up with. Everyone said that the monster Stocchino went around in the uniform of an infantryman, like a ghastly puppet with a grey-green cloak. Then they say that at a certain point she realised that what she saw was not a dream. They say she uttered a gasp, and that he too made a sound and put his finger to his lips as if to say "ssshhh". But Luigia Marianna opened her mouth to cry out so Samuele stabbed her right in the mouth. With a grimace like a broad grin the woman gained her feet and almost got away from him. Samuele had to chase after her and grasp her by the shoulders to turn her round and plunge the knife in again. She replied with a gurgle, felt she was vomiting blood, so she put a hand to her mouth and staggered two or three more steps towards the passage. But it was useless. In falling she left a fan of red blood on the wall. It occurred to Samuele that what was happening was a means of restoring some possibility of happiness to his life. What he felt within him could not be just written off as rage. It was like in war: men fall to the ground without so much as a sound . . . So it was that in the uproar of an artillery barrage, when the earth shook with the impact and all notion of perception vanished for a moment, then that was the time one fell. Looking around at that instant of silence, in the autumn of mortal bodies one could see soldiers falling like cards thrown down by a player who has lost. The sign of abomination is silence, overturning the world means dying in silence. In Emerenziano's house the real horror was the silence in which Pasquina, Giuseppe, Barbara and Luigia Marianna had left this world.

At last the master bedroom. On the wall the light of the full moon etched the elongated shadow of the arched bedhead. Samuele entered the room and sat down on a chair in a corner to watch the head of the family and his wife sleeping the sleep of the just. They had no inkling of the fearful maelstrom of events they had set in motion. Maybe this was the worst of their crimes, to have allowed themselves to be the innocent tools of evil. Look at them sleeping, yes, they could sleep, yet a long time ago they had refused water to a wayfarer. The question now was, what should be done? The just revenge would have been to let them sleep, to leave them alive to discover the slaughter when they woke. But that would have been cruel. So he stretched out his right hand to reach for his blade . . .

*

"It would have been cruel?" repeated Políto incredulously.

Samuele nodded. "Worse to let them live." Then he got to his feet. He was as frail and skeletal as a hanged man ravaged by the winds. Políto was the taller by inches, yet they managed to look each other in the eye. "I don't want to be forgiven and I don't want to forgive," said Samuele. The lamplight shed a golden glow on him. He seemed transparent, fairish-haired, with honey-coloured eyes, while his mouth was purplish and he had the fever of death upon him. "I still have some relations. If it was they who informed against me . . ."

"If they did, they could claim the reward. But not all of it, because that reward doesn't exist, Sergeant, it is only there for the honour . . . It's a put-up job."

"Very well," said Samuele. "It is as it should be, it's only there for the honour . . ."

"Your relations will get enough to enable them to live decently," Políto assured him.

But he was talking to thin air. Between one movement of the beam of light and the next, Samuele had vanished.

Políto bawled into the empty dark.

Samuele expected to be alone with the night-loving badger, expected a gust of wind to ruffle the alders. Expected to be able to understand that vast poem of columbines, arbutus and rock-roses. Then he reached the opening to his cave, with the sky of the Ogliastra so low it all but rested on his shoulders. And he realised that the space before him, above him and beneath him had become one tangible immensity. He realised that within that tangle, that fullness, that void, it was possible to give a name to things: to the breath of the earth, the odour of plants, the glitter of frost, the rustle of dead leaves. Ah, he realised that that wood was not a wood, but the entrance to an emptiness abstract but nonetheless familiar and intangibly substantial, like the memory of something that one has been and now no longer is. Like a lost certainty. A place from which we mortals have been expelled, a paradise we have not deserved. How many sons could say they had returned to the great mother, eh? How many could feel their own bodies as the product of the juices of that soil? This would have been a terrible memory. The inexplicable. There, for a bare instant, everything was clear, and clear also was the distance, and the waiting, and the times and places. There, within that memory of the abyss, when everything seems that it will happen and instead has already happened, Samuele Stocchino wept.

The hunter suddenly felt himself hunted by a deathly sense of futility. That feeling which in warfare he had often seen in the eyes of savage tribesmen, born to be sent out to die, or else in the futile spirallings of an insect. Right now he felt oppressed by that same futility. As if all his life long he had refused to understand that consciousness is a curse. Therefore those insect tribesmen had been born and had died in the world that had spawned them, the fruit of an awareness to which he had never had access until that very moment.

Then he realised that even that awareness was utterly futile, now that he was about to die.

The following day a young man arrived at the farm of one Cosimo Siotto, where Políto was bargaining over a consignment of Argentine grain. The young man, wearing traditional costume, had rather a long time to wait for the successful conclusion of the negotiations. Then, when he saw Políto making towards his horse, he raised his eyebrows to attract attention. Políto had noticed him earlier, but if there was one thing he had learned from the Sardinians it was that never, never must one give them any sort of advantage. So he had decided to let him wait as he went on play-acting as a corn merchant, keeping him in the corner of his eye.

Finally he replied to the other's gesture. The young man approached and introduced himself: "Vittorio Carta, son of Daniele. You will know who gave me this to pass on to you," he said, holding out a sealed envelope bearing Samuele's characteristically pointed handwriting. Políto seized it and pocketed it unopened.

When he did open it he found just what he was expecting: a day, a place and a sketched map.

Widow Cocco blew on the fingertips she had scorched on hot chestnuts. And she smiled a smile of surprise. What could be taking him off in the dead of night all the way to the cooper's house? she wondered. Saverio Políto gave a long look and chewed over a slow reply. He said that her story of the massacre had made such an impression on him that he wanted to go and see for himself. And what could he have seen there anyway? the widow Cocco wondered aloud. Just ruins . . . ruins . . .

"My job is finished," Políto said out of the blue. "Three more days at the most . . ." The woman stared at him, all attempt at speech frozen on her lips. "I must complete an order," he explained, "and then . . . I'm off."

Widow Cocco nodded as if this were something she already knew, but it was not so. That this man might leave had never even occurred to her. Such an oversight made her smile to herself a little.

"Do you want me to wash some things for you before you go?" she asked.

Políto said no. And then: "How do I get to S'Argiola 'e sa Perda?" he said a moment later, pronouncing the Sardinian words clumsily but exactly as if he had learned them by heart.

Widow Cocco gave him a long look. "It's not difficult," she replied.

213

EPILOGUE

With sadness at parting, but relief at the ending

At 5.00 a.m. Sergeant Palmas was throroughly intractable. All the more so because they loaded him, positively *loaded* him, onto some wreck of a vehicle left over from the war, along with Corporal Butto as driver and Commissioner Políto. Behind them, in the official car of the prefecture, came Cavaliere Dinale himself. It was a grey morning, of the kind that as children you remembered by the way they smelled. Such a morning as smells chilly, whatever the time of year. And in fact the sergeant shuddered to remember how many such mornings he had suffered going out to milk the ewes.

The jalopy lurched and lumbered round the hairpin bends on the way to Gairo. The sergeant watched as Corporal Butto drove with intense care . . . Políto looked straight ahead, with an expression of ruthless determination, on that hellish road as narrow and tangled as a skein of wool which the cat has been at.

"With all due respect, Your Excellency," the sergeant said at a certain point. Políto turned a fraction towards him to tacitly permit him to continue. "What do we have to conquer if we still have roads like this?"

Políto nodded with the ghost of a smile.

They were at six hundred metres above sea level before, just beyond the high point of Su Scrau, they began to descend until they reached a junction: Ulassai and Jerzu straight ahead, Ussassai to the right, Cardedu to the left. Políto was about to ask if there wasn't some mistake in those two almost identical signposts, but Butto chuckled quietly and went ahead, saying they were already there.

Well, almost. To get to S'Argiola 'e sa Perda they had a half-hour walk. So they left the cars on the dirt road and, much to the relief of Sergeant Palmas, set off on foot. Cavaliere Dinale chose to wait in the car.

Políto's map appeared to lead to a cave. Palmas had heard of it but never seen it, while Butto did not know much more about it than he did. The sketch included an unexpected detail: if you turned when you got to a massive oak with four great roots emerging above ground, then took twenty steps in the direction indicated by the largest root you reached a rocky place almost entirely hidden by bushes. Políto put his hand to his pistol and Palmas and Butto loaded their rifles, because at the very spot marked was the entrance to the cave.

The interior of the cave was surprisingly bright, lit by a number of torches which gave out a flickering, amber-coloured light. Everything in there looked as if it had been tidied by some loving hand. There were chairs and box seats, a table already laid up, a dresser, a crucifix and a number of well-ironed shirts stacked on a prie-dieu. There were piles of magazines and a desk with a pen, an inkpot and sheets of paper. There was a framed photograph of a smiling girl, with a pearl-grey ostrich feather stuck into the hook on which it hung.

Their hearts were in their mouths as they entered the bowels of the earth. There was not a sound, nothing. Nothing but the sense of a life secreted underground. The large, illuminated cavern narrowed to a fissure through which they could pass only in single file. Sergeant Palmas dared not open his mouth: he knew very well where they had got to, and so did Butto. They were both reluctant to enter the crevice, so Políto passed them and took the lead . . .

And so they found him. There was a bed, a chest of drawers,

a three-legged washstand with a mirror and on the marble top all the necessaries for shaving. On the floor beside the bed were a number of books, and on the bed lay Samuele. Políto felt his jugular with a forefinger to confirm what he had known at once.

"Dead," he said, to reassure Palmas and Butto who still had not dared to enter.

Palmas and Butto exchanged bewildered looks.

The three men carried him out to the clearing in front of the cave. Políto took him under the arms, and Palmas and Butto held a leg each, just as he had been carried as a child when they found him alive in the abyss. That came back to Palmas as a memory of his youth. He had only just been promoted to sergeant then and thought that in order to change things you had only to want to. To Butto it seemed quite unimaginable to be able to touch that body which had eluded everybody and too prosaic to think that the immortal was in fact dead forever. They then hurried through the woods, panting over the corpse, because that wreck of a man with his bleeding lips, who had seemed as frail as a rush when he was lying on the bed, was now heavier than expected.

The soil of S'Argola e' sa Perda is as violet as ox liver, or as the veils of oriental mourners, or as clotted blood . . . As violet as the colour of what we always wish to dream of because what we actally see is terrible, more terrible than any dream. That soil is more than mere soil, it is the dream of a kind of soil. It is slippery footing, the damp bed of a country stream . . .

As Palmas, Butto and Políto hauled along Samuele's dead weight, the further they went the more the soil sucked the body down, as if to reclaim it. Finally, out of breath and throwing caution to the wind, they practically dragged the body over the stones, brushing the low bushes, the nettles, the cardoons, the buds. That heaving, that panting, that slipping from the grasp, that gradual weakening of the elbows and knees, which little by little gave way to dragging him, look you: that was what they saw of the immortal, of Samuele Stocchino.

When they reached the middle of a clearing Políto ordered them to put him down. Before carrying him out of the cave they had laid on him his infantryman's cape. They now arranged his body at a spot indicated by Políto, so that it was half hidden by a bush.

Políto ran his eye over the scene, then turned to Corporal Butto and said: "You can shoot now." Butto stared at him as if he had not grasped what in fact he had grasped all too well. "Shoot him, Corporal," repeated Políto. Butto instinctively shook his head. "Shoot that man!" yelled Políto.

This time Butto levelled his rifle, his arms visibly shaking. The bullet struck the corpse on the ear, causing it to jump, but no blood came. Butto then dropped his rifle and fled to the rocks to be sick. Sergeant Palmas stared at Políto in amazement, but he realised there was a kind of ruthless understanding, almost of compassion, in that act of profanity. But when Políto looked at Palmas, the sergeant took a step back and shook his head. Políto thereupon wrenched the rifle from his hands, strode to the corpse, turned it face downwards and shot twice. The first bullet penetrated the loins and made the body give an odd leap with straddled legs. The second went into his thigh.

"He, at this point, evidently prevented from moving on account of the wounds in his thigh and loins, and having already fired the six cartridges with which his weapon was provided, took another cartridge clip from a leather bag he was wearing slung over one shoulder. I, Corporal Butto, profiting from the fact that the outlaw could at that moment make no use of his weapon, leaped from my hiding place, approached to some five metres from him and, pointing my rifle at his head, discharged a shot which struck the criminal in the left ear, stretching him lifeless."

"Lifeless," repeated the chancellor, to let Políto know that he could resume dictating. Prefect Dinale, expressionless, was smoking a cigar and standing at the half-open window of his office.

"Having confirmed the death of the outlaw, I, Sergeant Palmas, set a guard over the dead man who, on the evidence of the informer Vittorio Carta, was at once identified as the above-mentioned fugitive from justice, Samuele Stocchino . . ."

"Vittorio Carta?" broke in the chancellor with a glance at Prefect Dinale. "I should point out that Vittorio Carta would in this case have a right to the price set on Stocchino's head."

Políto made a gesture of impatience and Dinale told his subordinate to carry on. But the latter stubbornly insisted: "Vittorio Carta is a first cousin of Stocchino's, so that the reward . . . Your Excellency . . .", he pleaded, turning to address Dinale. But Políto brought his fist down on the table. The chancellor gave a start and Dinale told him to carry on.

"Where were we?" enquired Políto wearily.

" . . . was identified as the above-mentioned fugitive Samuele Stocchino . . ." spelled out the chancellor, fuming with rage.

"We thereupon immediately dispatched Officer Antonio Toro to the carabinieri station in Gairo, which was the closest . . ."

"The man was not even on the scene," put in the chancellor once more. "This is a total put-up job!" he exclaimed, revealing truly notable insight.

" . . . to make the due report to the party officials and the judicial authorities!" yelled Políto. "The latter, on reaching the scene in the evening to make the inspection proper to their role, ordered the removal of the body which was confirmed to be that of the dangerous fugitive Samuele Stocchino, aged . . . How old was he?" asked Políto, turning to the others.

Dinale merely shrugged.

"Thirty-nine, perhaps?" The chancellor replied with another question.

"Write down thirty-nine. Thirty-nine years old, from Arzana."

And so they declared that Samuele was dead. But try telling that to the locals. No, not him. He had gone through the entire excursus of sainthood. As they say in the lives of the saints: in youth a sinner, a bravo, a braggart and a boozer; in manhood a mystic, devout, valiant and virtuous. He had been dead and buried, but he rose again.

What, *him* dead? No, no. Not *him*!

Well, work it out as best you may.

AFTERWORD

Samuele Stochino is a historical character, though at the same time legendary.

Samuele Stocchino (with double "c") is the twice-over legendary character whose story is told in these pages.

What you have read is not the truth. Real names and false names serve the purpose of telling a story while pretending it is true, whereas it is only partly so, or not at all.

My thanks go to Franco Fresi and Lina Aresu, without whose true stories I would not have been able to invent this one.

MARCELLO FOIS was born in Sardinia in 1960 and is one of a gifted group of writers called "Group 13", who explore the cultural roots of their various regions. He writes for the theatre, television and cinema, and is the author several novels, including *The Advocate* (2003).

PATRICK CREAGH is the award-winning translator of Antonio Tabucchi, Salvatore Satta, Italo Calvino, Flavio Conti, Gesualdo Bufalino and Claudio Magris.